Dark Secret

Dark
Secret

MARINA
ANDERSON

sphere

SPHERE

First published in Great Britain in 1995 by X Libris
This paperback edition published in 2012 by Sphere
Reprinted 2012 (twice)

Copyright © 1995 by Marina Anderson

The moral right of the author has been asserted.

A CIP catalogue record for this book
is available from the British Library.

ISBN 978-0-7515-5100-6

Typeset in Sabon by M Rules
Printed and bound in Great Britain by
Clays Ltd, St Ives plc

Papers used by Sphere are from well-managed forests
and other responsible sources.

MIX
Paper from
responsible sources
FSC® C104740

Sphere
An imprint of
Little, Brown Book Group
100 Victoria Embankment
London EC4Y 0DY

An Hachette UK Company
www.hachette.co.uk

www.littlebrown.co.uk

Dark Secret

Chapter One

'HARRIET, WHERE'S YOUR ring?' asked Ella, her RADA trained voice carrying to every corner of the wine bar.

Harriet blushed and removed her left hand from the top of the table, sliding it out of sight beneath the table-cloth. 'Keep your voice down,' she muttered.

'But where is it?' persisted Ella. 'Surely the ever-efficient Miss Radcliffe hasn't mislaid her impeccably tasteful and priceless engagement ring? What on earth will James say?' she added.

'James won't be worried. I've given it back to him,' said Harriet.

Ella stared at her friend in astonishment and then

drained her glass. It was her usual reaction to any kind of shock. 'You mean, you're not going to marry James after all?'

Harriet nodded. 'That's what I mean.'

'But why? You were the perfect couple, and with you at his side James would have gone right to the top. God, I wish I could find a merchant banker to marry me, I can tell you.'

Despite her depression, Harriet laughed. 'Ella, you could never marry anyone like James. You'd die of boredom on your honeymoon.'

'Really?' Ella leant forward eagerly. 'You mean you're finally going to confess the secrets of your sex life together? Wasn't he any good in bed?'

Harriet shrugged. 'He was all right. I mean, he was always very considerate and made sure I was satisfied, it was just that there was never any ...' I don't know, excitement really. I suppose he loved me, but he lacked real passion. I was in bed with him last Saturday and when he turned on his side and his hand went straight to the same place as it always did I suddenly thought, I can't stand this any more; if he touches me there one more time I shall scream. Well, he touched me and I did.'

'You screamed?' Ella was stunned.

Harriet laughed. 'Yes! I actually screamed *"Don't do that"* at him. I felt terrible afterwards. He was so hurt, and kept saying "but I thought you liked it", which I did the first few times. Anyway, that was it really. He said I must be having a breakdown and needed a rest. I said it wasn't that at all; it was simply that I'd finally come to my senses and realised he wasn't the man for me. Then I gave him back his ring and he left. End of story.'

'But the wedding!' exclaimed Ella. 'All those guests, and the presents you've already had.'

Harriet nodded. 'I know. Luckily since my parents are still abroad and weren't even coming they won't kick up a fuss. It's poor James who'll have to cope with his family's wrath.'

'Have you told them at work?' asked Ella.

'There wasn't any need. I went in to work on the Monday and handed in my notice.'

'Get another bottle of wine,' said Ella. 'This is too much to cope with sober. I mean to say, Harriet, we've known each other for over ten years and in all that time you've never done anything unexpected. You passed all your exams easily, got a wonderful job in the City as PA to a top company director, became engaged to a handsome, wealthy merchant banker and were just about to marry him and produce the requisite son and daughter – in the correct order no doubt – and then you decide to go totally off the rails. That's *my* prerogative. I'm the actress, I'm the one who does outrageous things and you always listen and give me good advice that I ignore. How come our roles have been reversed?'

Harriet's hands twisted together in her lap. 'I don't know. Like I say, it just happened out of the blue. I mean, there has to be more to life, Ella, doesn't there?'

'More what?' enquired Ella, pouring herself a glass of wine from the second bottle. 'Money? Sex? Career? Which particular rejected aspect of your wonderful life were you hoping to improve on?'

'All of them,' confessed Harriet.

Ella looked at her friend. At twenty-three she was a tall, slim, leggy brunette with grey eyes and a cool air of self-possession. This evening, as always, she was dressed impeccably, in a suit with a long-line jacket that ended three inches above the hem of her skirt and a knotted cream silk scarf at her throat. Her appearance suited her life, or the life she'd led until now. Suddenly Ella wondered what hidden depths there were to her friend.

'Right then,' she said briskly. 'If you want to improve them all, where do you intend to start?'

'I want an interesting job; something really different,' declared Harriet.

'Any ideas?'

Harriet pulled a face. 'That's the trouble, I can't think what I want to do, I only know that it has to be exciting and different.'

'Try being an actress,' suggested Ella. 'There's plenty of excitement there. Will I be working this time next week or not!'

Harriet sighed. 'I know I've probably been stupid but I simply couldn't stop myself. It was as though a voice in my head was telling me that this was my last chance. If I didn't stop now, change direction quickly, it would be too late.'

'Stupid or not, you've done it,' said Ella. 'Have you looked for a job yet?'

'I glanced through some adverts in the evening paper, but there wasn't anything that appealed to me. There are several jobs like the one that I had, but there's no point in that.'

Ella dived into the large canvas bag that she always carried around with her. 'Let's see what I've got here.

The Stage – well that's no good to you, you haven't got an Equity card! *Evening Standard* – you've seen that; *The Times* – let's try that.'

'That won't have anything exciting,' protested Harriet, but Ella was already scanning the situations vacant column, muttering to herself as her eyes raced over the words.

'Hey, this looks promising,' she exclaimed suddenly. 'Listen Harriet. "American actress on six-month stay in England needs PA of sociable disposition who is willing to work unusual hours. CV and photograph essential." Then there's a box number for replies. What do you think?'

'It's a PA job again,' said Harriet doubtfully.

'Hardly the same as working in the City,' Ella pointed out. 'It might be Meryl Streep or Sharon Stone. How fantastic to see them at close quarters!'

'Don't be silly,' aid Harriet. 'They wouldn't need to put an advert in *The Times*. Besides, why do I have to send a photograph?'

'I don't know. Perhaps the actress has a fragile ego and doesn't want any competition. You could be too good-looking for the job.'

Harriet laughed. 'I doubt it. If anyone was likely to

put a film star's nose out of joint it would be you, not me.'

Ella studied her friend and silently disagreed. She knew that she was attractive, and with make-up could look beautiful, but there was something special about Harriet, something that had always made people look twice. She was so immaculate, so apparently assured and yet in her eyes, and her body language, there was quite often the suggestion that beneath this surface there lay something more. A vulnerability certainly, but also the very quality that Harriet herself had said James lacked – passion. An untapped passion, as Ella knew very well, was an irresistible aphrodisiac to a lot of men.

'I think you should answer the advert,' she said decisively. 'You've nothing to lose.'

Harriet felt her stomach move with nervous excitement. It would be exciting, and different, but she also sensed something more from the wording of the advertisement. Somehow she knew that if she sent off a photograph and was given an interview her whole life would change, and she hesitated because if that happened there would be no going back.

'Well?' demanded Ella impatiently.

Harriet hesitated for only a second. 'You've convinced me,' she agreed with a nervous laugh. 'I'll send off a photo and my CV tomorrow.'

'No, tonight,' said Ella firmly. 'We'll go back to your place and I'll help you choose the best picture, then we'll make sure it goes first post tomorrow.'

That night, as Harriet prepared for bed, she thought for a moment about the letter, now lying in a pillar box awaiting the postman in the morning. Would anything come of it? she thought to herself. Had her meeting with Ella and the fact that she'd had a copy of *The Times* with her been part of some predestined plan? Or would she hear nothing more and spend the next few months wondering if she'd been right to give up James and her job in the space of three days? She rather suspected it would be the latter, but couldn't help nurturing a hope that at least she'd manage to get an interview, if only in order to find out who the actress in question was.

Two days later she returned from visiting a friend to find her telephone ringing. She ran to answer it.

'Miss Radcliffe?' asked an icily detached female voice at the other end.

'Yes,' replied Harriet, somewhat mystified as to who the called could be.

'You replied to an advertisement in *The Times* recently.'

Harriet's stomach lurched. 'Yes, yes I did.'

'Your CV and photograph were satisfactory. Would you be free to attend an interview tomorrow morning at eleven?' asked the voice.

Harriet felt flustered. 'Tomorrow? Let me see, I ...'

'Tomorrow is the only time that our client has free.'

'I'm sure it will be fine. I'll just check my diary,' replied Harriet, determined not to let the caller know that at this particular moment she had nothing planned for the rest of her life. She waited a couple of minutes and then returned to the phone. 'Yes, I can manage that,' she said, hoping she sounded as indifferent as the other woman.

'Excellent, I'll give you the address. Do you have a pen and paper to hand?'

She must think I'm six years old, thought Harriet to herself, but she kept the annoyance out of her voice and scribbled down the address and directions as to how to get there. It was only when she replaced the receiver that her legs went weak and she had to sit on the sofa to recover.

It was all so quick, she thought in astonishment. An advertisement like that must have attracted masses of applications, and yet she'd been called by phone in less than forty-eight hours. The speed of the response made her nervous and later that evening she rang Ella.

'Why are you worrying?' Ella demanded. 'You should be grateful. Where do you have to go?'

'Regent's Park. I've looked it up on the map – I think it's one of those large houses that overlook the park.'

'Fantastic! You'll probably have your own suite of rooms and use of a swimming pool – when the star isn't keeping in trim, of course. Did they say who she was?'

'No, but no doubt I'll find out early on in the interview.'

'Make sure you let me know,' said Ella. 'I'm consumed with curiosity.'

'So am I,' responded Harriet.

By the time she actually arrived at the house the following morning she was consumed by nerves as well. She drove herself there in her blue BMW which had to stop at the huge padlocked wrought-iron gates while a gateman came out, took her name and phoned through to the house. Then he opened them with apparent reluctance and when she waved and smiled at him as she drove in he simply stared blankly at her. 'Let's hope the rest of the household are more friendly,' she muttered to herself.

The house was large and imposing. It was built of Portland stone and stood well back in what Harriet estimated to be about two to three acres of parkland. When she halted her car outside the front door she looked down across an immaculate lawn with green conifers and bushes on either side extended right back to the gates. As far as she could see, the garden at the side was less well tended and comprised more shrubs than lawn, but the entire perimeter of the area was protected by tall trees which successfully shut out the rest of the world.

A butler opened the front door to her, and she stepped into a long entrance hall, at the far end of which she could see a modern open-plan winding staircase. The carpet was a deep coral colour, the walls and ceiling a textured white and on either side of the hall there were numerous china and porcelain ornaments ranging from a life-size greyhound sitting to attention to an exquisitely delicate ballerina which was little more than six inches in height and stood on an ornate glass table. The ornaments had no apparent connection with each other and none of them matched in colour or design but Harriet suspected that every one of them was priceless.

'If you would wait here, Miss Radcliffe,' said the butler politely, ushering her into a tiny ante-room. 'Miss Farmer will be with you in a moment.'

Harriet sat down on the nearest chair and wondered if she could possibly have heard him right. If Miss Farmer was her possible future employer then there was only one person it could be. Rowena Farmer, who had shot to fame in two huge box office successes as a sexy private investigator, becoming at the same time one of the greatest sex symbols since Marilyn Monroe. Harriet's heart began to beat more rapidly, but then she told herself firmly that Miss Farmer was probably a secretary whose job it was to weed out unsuitable applicants. It was hardly likely that someone like Rowena Farmer would do her own interviewing.

Just as she'd calmed her nerves the door opened and Rowena Farmer made her entrance. There was no other expression that applied, thought Harriet to herself, as the petite titian-haired beauty stood framed in the doorway. Dressed in a canary yellow cropped top and a bronze organdie skirt with a pale green sleeveless overtop that reached to her ankles she stood directly in the light from the opposite window, her hair gleaming and her immaculately made-up face glowing with health, and smiled a brilliant, professional smile at Harriet.

'I'm so sorry to have kept you waiting, Miss Radcliffe,' she murmured in the famous low husky voice that Harriet recognised from her films. 'There's so much to do at the moment. We only arrived three days ago and ... well, you can imagine what it's like, I'm sure.'

Again she smiled, but Harriet knew that the smile wasn't really for her. It was an automatic response to another person's presence, and as such meaningless, but at least she was being polite. Somehow Harriet had expected her to be spoilt and petulant in private. Then she reminded herself that this wasn't in private. Rowena Farmer was performing for a possible employee. The real Miss Farmer was unlikely to emerge until you were actually in her employment.

'Come this way,' continued the film star, gliding smoothly out into the hall, and Harriet followed her to the far end and then through a heavy oak door into a drawing-room.

The carpet here was pure white, while the walls were white with the faintest suggestion of apple green, a tone that was complimented by the low green sofa and two winged chairs. In the middle of the room a large glass table top was supported by four green chinese dragons whose images were repeated in the draped and tied curtains that had been fastened in such a way as to allow in only a very little light.

Rowena Farmer sank into one of the chairs and indicated that Harriet should sit on the sofa. It was lower than normal and she wished that she'd worn a longer skirt as hers rose above her thighs and left her sitting with her knees tightly together and angled to her left. She still had the suspicion that Rowena Farmer must be able to see right up her skirt if she wanted to, but the film star's eyes never left Harriet's face until she picked up the application and read it through as though to remind herself of its contents.

At the far end of the drawing-room, directly opposite Harriet, was an ornate mirror that took up half the wall. She smiled to herself. Probably film stars liked mirrors everywhere, and certainly Rowena Farmer had every cause to be proud of her beauty, which was as spectacular in the flesh as on the screen.

While Harriet tried to sit still and Rowena read her CV, a man sitting concealed behind the mirror glanced down at the written notes on the table in front of him. His long fingers picked up a pen and he began to scribble comments in the margins of the pages, and all the time he watched the unsuspecting Harriet through the two-way mirror. Beneath heavy dark brows his brown eyes gleamed with appreciation.

After what seemed to be a very long time, Rowena put the letter of application to one side and turned her attention to Harriet. 'Why did you leave your last job?' she enquired.

Harriet had already decided to be completely honest. 'I was bored,' she confessed. 'The work was interesting at first but it quickly became routine. The money was good and so were the working conditions, but I needed a change. I wanted to do something where every day would be slightly different. I was doing a lot of figure work you see, and I really prefer people.' She smiled at Rowena, but the film star didn't smile back. Her eyes were quite blank, as though she didn't understand what Harriet was saying.

Harriet felt she had to explain further, because she wanted this job very badly. The thought of actually working for someone as famous as Rowena Farmer was irresistible. 'I was engaged until recently, but I realised that the engagement was rather like my job, agreeable but unexciting. I was afraid that if I didn't change, didn't try something different – broaden my horizons more – I'd end up regretting it.'

'You want to broaden your horizons?' queried Rowena with sudden interest.

'Yes!' said Harriet eagerly. 'I'm twenty-three now; soon it will be too late.'

'Twenty-three is young,' murmured the film star regretfully.

'But it's so easy to settle for too little,' said Harriet, warming to her theme. 'Ever since I was young I've thought that it was being safe that mattered. Everything I did was carefully thought out, and if there was ever any risk, any chance of something going wrong, I discarded that option. Now I think I was wrong, and I want to do something different with my life while I still can.'

'You're looking for danger?'

Behind the mirror the man leant forward slightly, his chin resting on his hands. This was going far better than he could ever have anticipated. So far she was perfect.

Harriet smiled. 'Not danger in the way of climbing rock faces or sailing round the world in a yacht, but I'd like to take a chance or two before I settle down.'

Rowena nodded. 'And at the moment do you have any emotional attachments?'

The hidden man almost stopped breathing as he waited for Harriet's answer. If she said yes then she would be of no use to them, and he desperately wanted her to join their household.

Harriet shook her head. 'There's no one. I'm not in a hurry to replace James. In fact, I'm enjoying the feeling of freedom!'

Rowena laughed, but again Harriet had the disconcerting impression that it was a professional laugh. This woman wasn't amused, and in a way she hardly seemed interested enough in what Harriet was saying. She put the questions, but then her attention seemed to wander and she would stare over Harriet's shoulder and out of the window rather than at her face.

'The thing is Harriet – I may call you Harriet, I hope?' Harriet nodded. 'Good. The thing is that I'm here to make a very special film, and it's vital that no word of this gets out until everything is settled. You know – script, cast, contracts signed, all those boring things that have to be done before you can be sure a project is underway.'

'I'm afraid I don't know anything about the way the film industry works,' confessed Harriet.

Rowena shrugged dismissively. 'That doesn't matter, you'd soon learn. No, what I need is a discreet, efficient English secretary. They're famous for their discretion and efficiency, you know. Unfortunately, in order to fit in with my rather demanding schedule it would be necessary for the successful applicant to live in for the length of my stay here.'

'Live in?' said Harriet in astonishment.

'It's the time difference, darling,' explained Rowena, longing to light up a cigarette but aware that Lewis, watching from behind the mirror, would disapprove. 'You'd get telephone calls at all hours. Also, I suffer from insomnia-sometimes I'd want to dictate letters in the middle of the night if I couldn't sleep.'

Harriet stared at the other woman. She'd have thought that a fax machine would have taken care of night-time calls, and as for insomnia, everyone knew that film stars lived on sleeping pills, but she wasn't going to argue. It was a beautiful house and the job was only for six months. She had no objection to living in.

She could easily go back to her own flat now and again, during her time off, and make sure everything there was secure. Just the same, it was a strange request.

'I'd pay double your previous salary,' said Rowena suddenly.

Harriet tried not to let her astonishment show. She'd been very well paid in her previous job; doubling it when she was going to live in was extraordinary.

'To make up for the inconvenience of losing your social life for six months,' explained Rowena. 'I doubt if you'll have much free time. I'm afraid I'm very demanding!' Again the practised laugh.

'But I would have time off?' queried Harriet.

'Of course, although not necessarily set days. It's so difficult in this business to know when you'll need someone and when you won't. You do understand?'

'Yes, of course. It's just all rather strange to me, I'm afraid.'

Rowena curled her legs under her in the chair, looking frail and kittenish. 'But surely that's what you wanted, Harriet? A change. Something that would broaden your horizons. I can certainly promise you that.'

Go for it, said a voice in Harriet's head. You wanted

a chance to experience new things and this is it. Why are you hanging back? She gave herself a mental shake. 'It sounds very exciting,' she said with a laugh.

Rowena seemed to relax suddenly, and let out her breath with an audible sigh. 'That's great, Harriet. Naturally there are one or two points I have to check up on. References, that kind of thing, but I'm sure we won't come across any problems there. With any luck I can let you know definitely by the end of tomorrow.'

As Harriet rose to her feet and let Rowena usher her out of the room she wondered briefly who the 'we' was. She had no idea if Rowena was married or not, and decided that if she got the job she must ring Ella and find out all she could about the woman she'd be working for.

As they reached the front door the butler materialised, but Rowena waved him away and opened the door herself. She then extended a small, perfectly manicured hand to Harriet. 'I'm sure you'd fit in very well here, Harriet,' she said with the warmest smile she'd managed during the entire interview. 'I do so admire cool English women. I'm afraid we're rather more upfront in the States.'

'Maybe you're just more friendly,' suggested Harriet.

'I trust that if you do join us you won't find our way of life too overwhelming,' responded Rowena. 'Not that it will matter. As you said, you wanted a change.'

Harriet smiled and made her way to her car. She had a sneaking suspicion that instead of cool, Rowena Farmer had actually meant boring or inhibited, but it didn't bother her. She wanted the job, and she couldn't imagine a similar opportunity ever coming her way again. She just hoped that the film star thought she was suitable.

The film star in question watched the BMW draw away from the house and leant against the wall, totally drained by her own performance. She'd woken that morning exhausted and sated by a night of love-making, her head throbbing from an excess of champagne, and she'd completely forgotten about Harriet until twenty minutes before she arrived. Even then it was only fear of her husband's fury that had driven her to leave her bed and she'd then bullied and cajoled her dresser into getting her ready on time.

Slowly she returned to the drawing-room where the interview had taken place. Lewis was already there, lounging in the second armchair, his long legs stretched out in front of him. She stood on the threshold of the room and studied him carefully. At thirty-nine he was even more attractive now than when she'd met him four years earlier and she thought how unfair it was that men improved with the years while women didn't – at least not film stars who built their reputations on looks and glamour.

Lewis was going to change all that though. This new film, his brainchild and as such a guaranteed box office success, would show people that she was more than a sex symbol. That she could show depth and passion, and she was willing to bare her soul in order to regain her place in the hall of fame. She was scared, but Lewis would help her.

He turned his head. 'You did well,' he said slowly.

Rowena sat down in her chair and with trembling hands reached for the cigarettes in her handbag. She heard him sigh but ignored him. There were times, moments like this, when the danger of what they were doing overwhelmed her and she had to have help. He'd weaned her off her drugs, restricted her drinking but had so far failed to get her to give up smoking. Sometimes his almost puritanical approach to certain aspects of life irritated her, but she knew that it made him what he was and was responsible for his incredible success.

'She's the one, isn't she?' commented Rowena, drawing on the cigarette.

'She could have stepped straight from the pages of the script,' agreed Lewis. 'It's incredible. Those long legs, that fantastic air of self-contained reserve with the suggestion of so much more beneath. And those eyes! Did you see them? They reveal everything she tries to conceal. I can't wait to begin.'

Rowena couldn't remember when she'd last seen her husband so enthusiastic. 'What about Chris?' she asked.

He raised his eyebrows. 'Chris will go along with our decision. I bore his preferences in mind when I made out my list of essential requirements.'

'I'm not sure she'll stay, even if she takes the job,' said Rowena.

'She'll stay.' Lewis sounded supremely confident and it annoyed his wife.

'When she said she wanted to broaden her horizons I'm not sure she meant them to expand quite as far as you intend.'

'It will all be done very slowly,' Lewis reminded her.

'By the time she realises what's happening she'll be too involved to leave. Trust me, Rowena. If there's one thing I do know about, apart from making films, it's women.'

Rowena knew this was true. She'd had a lot of men herself, but never anyone like Lewis. He was everything she could ever have asked for, totally uninhibited and unashamed, prepared to go to any lengths to satisfy her needs and desires. Yet even that wasn't enough, she thought bitterly. Even Lewis with his intelligence, good looks and sexual skill had been unable to help her. Which was why they were here, and why they needed Harriet.

'Ring her tomorrow at six o'clock,' said Lewis, getting out of his chair and taking the half-smoked cigarette from between his wife's fingers. 'By then she'll be worrying that you're not going to call and should accept straight away. Now get back to bed, you look exhausted. And do stop smoking these things. They don't help your skin or your nerves and I loathe the smell.'

'Just because all your films are moral crusades, do you have to carry it over into your private life?' enquired Rowena irritably.

Lewis smiled. 'You more than anyone should know that I'm not quite what people think!'

'Sometimes I'm not sure I know you at all,' retorted Rowena.

Lewis reached forward and stroked her left cheek softly with the middle finger of his right hand. 'You know all you need to know,' he murmured. 'Now go and rest. I have to work on the script.'

'Is it all right if I show her photograph to Chris?' asked Rowena.

'No,' said Lewis sharply. 'I don't want him to set eyes on her until she's actually living in this house.'

They both knew that Rowena wouldn't disobey him, because if she did then the delicate balance of the script would be changed, and the script was entirely Lewis's responsibility.

At five past six the following evening the telephone rang in Harriet's apartment. She had been pacing back and forth in front of it for the past half hour and almost snatched it off the rest in her haste. 'Hello?'

'Miss Radcliffe?' asked the husky voice of Rowena Farmer.

'Yes,' said Harriet, eagerly.

'I'm delighted to say that all your references checked out satisfactorily and I'd like to offer you the job,' said Rowena.

Harriet felt almost light-headed with excitement. The few things that had been troubling her, any doubts as to the wisdom of such a change, vanished in the wave of relief that the job was hers, just as Lewis had anticipated.

'Are you still interested?' Rowena sounded anxious, and Harriet realised that she hadn't said a word yet.

'Yes, yes of course!' she exclaimed. 'I'm really pleased.'

'So are we,' responded Rowena, and again Harriet wondered about her use of the word *we*. 'I was wondering if you could start next week? I didn't bring my secretary with me and the correspondence is already beginning to pile up.'

'Of course,' said Harriet swiftly. 'I have to make a few arrangements about the flat, but I could certainly start next Monday.'

'And you'll bring all you need then?'

'Well, yes.'

'I realised I didn't show you your rooms,' said Rowena, sounding embarrassed by her own error. 'If you wanted to come and have a look before Monday that could easily be arranged. You'll have your own bedroom, bathroom and living-room on the first floor. The rooms are all large here; I'm sure you'll find them acceptable.'

Remembering what she'd seen of the house so far, Harriet couldn't imagine otherwise. 'I'm sure they'll be perfect,' she assured Rowena. 'Honestly, I don't need to come and look.'

'Well, if there's anything you don't like we can always have it changed,' responded the film star. In the short pause that followed Harriet heard another voice, a man's deep and soft, almost like a whisper. 'Oh, yes!' exclaimed Rowena. 'There is one little thing I forgot. I'm afraid you won't be able to have visitors here. It's the film, you see. Everything is at such a delicate stage that I don't want any word to escape and if . . .'

'It's all right,' Harriet assured her. 'I can always go out to see my friends. Really, there's no problem.'

'I'm so glad you understand.' The relief in Rowena's voice was clear and for a moment Harriet felt sorry for her, although she couldn't imagine why. 'We'll see you on Monday morning then, let's say at eleven-thirty. The household should be awake at that time!'

'Fine,' said Harriet. 'And thank you.'

'I should be thanking you,' said Rowena softly, and then she hung up.

As Harriet started to dial Ella's number, Rowena turned to Lewis, who had been standing at her elbow throughout the call. 'There, it's settled,' she said triumphantly.

He nuzzled the nape of her neck while his arms wound themselves round her body and his hands caressed her breasts through the flimsy material of her blouse. 'Well done,' he murmured. 'Now we can begin.'

They sank on to the carpet together and as his cool, clever fingers played over her warm flesh her last coherent thought was to wonder what Chris would think of their choice.

Chapter Two

ON THE MONDAY morning, as Harriet packed the last of her belongings into suitcases, Rowena stirred sleepily in her four-poster bed. Lewis had awoken earlier, she'd heard him dress and leave, and remembering that today was an important one for them all Rowena decided that perhaps she should join him for a cup of coffee and some fruit juice before dressing.

She opened her eyes, but not a glimmer of light penetrated the room. Still half-asleep she turned her head towards the window, and realised with a shiver of excitement that she was wearing a blindfold. Instinctively she tried to move her hands, to test exactly what had been used to cover her eyes, but immediately a pair of wiry hands gripped her wrists, pinning them to her pillow.

'Chris, stop it!' she protested half-heartedly. 'I have to get up this morning. Harriet will be here soon.'

'I want to know about Harriet,' he whispered in her ear, his breath warm against her skin. 'Tell me what she looks like. Is she beautiful? Will I want her enough for the plot to work?'

'I can't tell you,' she explained, twisting her body in her efforts to free herself. Chris grasped her legs and pushed them roughly upwards so that her knees were bent against her ample breasts and then she felt him move over her until her ankles were on his shoulders and his erection was resting against her. She knew that she was already moist, already wanting him, and knew that Chris was aware of it too because he laughed softly deep in his throat.

'Tell me,' he taunted her, letting the tip of his penis brush lightly up and down her slowly parting outer sex-lips. 'Tell me about Harriet and then you can have me.'

'I can't! repeated Rowena, wishing that she could just so that she could feel him hard and urgent inside her.

Chris rotated his hips slightly and she felt the soft tip

of his penis caressing the sensitive nerve endings around her clitoris. Immediately she tried to arch herself upwards to increase the stimulation but her movements were restricted by the position he'd chosen and she whimpered with frustration.

Suddenly he withdrew from between her legs, pressed her legs down flat on the-bed, then lay on top of her, his hands going to her breasts. Still unable to see, Rowena's breathing increased as she waited for his next move. She could feel her body trembling with need, a need mixed with the glorious fear that Chris always aroused in her. A fear that she had grown to need, to rely on for her greatest moments of pleasure.

Very softly his fingers closed round her right breast. They skimmed lightly over the surface and Rowena's lips parted as she waited for what was to come. Very gradually, with tantalising slowness, his fingers moved across the surface of the rounded breast until it reached the aureola. Then the finger nails scratched lightly at the most sensitive part of the film star's breasts and as her nipple rose with her increased excitement Chris lowered his head and sucked it into his mouth.

The pressure combined with the insistent scratching meant that Rowena's hips twisted on the bed as she sought some kind of contact against the lower half of her body, but Chris moved to the side of her, denying her stimulation of any kind.

'Tell me what Harriet looks like,' he repeated and she could have cried because when he spoke he released her imprisoned nipple from his mouth.

'No!' She made her voice firmer, aware that no matter what he did this time he wasn't going to have his way and he might as well know it now.

'Why do you let him do this to us?' whispered Chris, and to her amazement and gratitude she felt one of his hands straying between her thighs, idly caressing the soft, damp, swollen flesh. 'We're not social misfits, or politicians. He should stick to his dramatised documentaries, not use us to launch him into fiction.'

'It isn't fiction,' Rowena said softly. 'It's faction. That's why we're so necessary, and I need this film, Chris. I need it badly. I'm thirty now, I can't rely on my looks any more. I have to show that I can act.'

'This isn't acting,' exclaimed Chris, and behind the darkness of the blindfold, Rowena was startled by the sudden insertion into her vagina of a gently rounded vibrator that Chris immediately switched on to the higher setting.

As its pulsations spread through her, as her outer nerve endings were stimulated by the strength of the movements within her, Rowena's body began to climb to orgasm. She felt her nipples standing erect, felt the hot melting sensation deep within the core of her and when Chris's spare hand gripped her right breast, her head began to move almost imperceptibly on the pillow and she heard herself moaning.

'Do you want me instead of this toy?' he asked, his own voice trembling with excitement.

'Yes! Yes, please Chris, now! Quickly!' Rowena was frantic to feel him inside her, to know that he was there when she finally toppled into orgasm.

'Then tell me about Harriet,' he demanded.

Rowena's stomach was rigid with sexual tension and her thighs began to shake as the orgasm drew closer. 'Please, Chris, I can't. Just take me, take me now.'

'Bitch!' he muttered, and to her horror the vibrator was withdrawn, her breast released and the blissful sparks began to die away. Without thinking Rowena's own hand moved between her thighs, to finish what Chris had so abruptly ended, but his hands stopped her and he kept her imprisoned flat on the bed, still unable to see because of the blindfold, and only released her when her body had finally returned to its former unaroused state. Then he pulled off the dark scarf and stared down at her.

'You shouldn't have done that!' cried Rowena. 'It wasn't fair.'

'You and Lewis shouldn't have chosen Harriet without asking my opinion.'

'He's my husband and the director of the film, whereas you're—'

'Just a small-part actor?' he queried.

'No, of course not, but he has to run this his way. He wants it to be as accurate as possible, that's why we need Harriet. He chose the characters and he wants to see how they really react to the situation his film characters will face. Don't you see how real it will make it? No one will be able to say "that's not how people behave" because we'll already have behaved like it. We *are* his film.'

'He's trying to get rid of me,' said Chris.

Rowena reached up to brush his fair curly hair out of his eyes. 'He could never do that, Chris,' she assured him. 'I couldn't live without you, you know that and Lewis knows it too.'

Chris leant over her and kissed her deeply, his tongue

thrusting into her mouth just as she'd wanted his erection to thrust a few minutes earlier. Her arms went round his neck and she arched up so that her nipples brushed the soft down on his chest. 'Please, let's do it now,' she begged him.

'No,' said Chris curtly, and he pushed her off the bed. 'Get dressed. Your husband's probably waiting for you.'

'Sometimes I hate you,' said Rowena, refusing to let herself cry because it would ruin her looks for the rest of the morning.

Chris laughed. 'It didn't look that way earlier.'

'What's wrong with us?' demanded Rowena. 'Why can't we be ...'

'Normal?' enquired Chris. He smiled his most boyish smile. 'I've no idea. Perhaps Lewis will discover the answer as the plot unravels.'

Harriet was surprised when Rowena Farmer opened the front door to her in person. Now that she'd accepted the job she hadn't expected the film star to bother to be even professionally friendly. Ella had made it quite clear over the telephone that this star in particular was one who took her position as a sex goddess very seriously.

'She wants to be known as an "actress" too,' Ella had informed her friend. 'That's probably why she's here. The Americans think that the best serious films are made in England. Incidentally,' Ella had added, 'Ms Farmer just happens to be married to the hottest director in the States at the moment, and I mean hot. He's the new Oliver Stone and incredibly handsome. I saw him once on a clip of film showing them together and one glimpse made my knees go weak!'

'I don't suppose I'll see much of him,' Harriet had responded, and then thought very little more about it.

Now though, as Rowena motioned for a waiting maid to take Harriet's suitcases and then led her through to the drawing-room she remembered Ella's words, because Rowena was talking about her husband.

'You must meet Lewis before I show you your rooms,' she said gaily. 'He's usually locked away in his study working on the script or talking on the telephone, but I've told him that when you're not busy with my work he can borrow you – I didn't think you'd mind – so he's taken time out to meet you.'

Harriet had the feeling that Rowena felt this was a great honour, but she found it hard to feel overwhelmed. It was after all only courtesy to say hello to someone who was going to type your letters and probably be a general dogsbody.

She followed Rowena into the room and immediately the man sitting in the chair opposite the door rose to his feet. He was tall, an inch or so over six feet, Harriet thought, and his hair was thick and jet black, swept off his face, accentuating the unusually strong bone structure with its high cheekbones and straight nose. Beneath dark and heavy brows his eyes were a deep brown, thickly lashed and intelligent-looking while his mouth was wide with a full lower lip. He held out a hand in greeting, and the leather strap of his watch stood out against his golden brown skin. Harriet remembered Ella mentioning mixed parentage – a Portuguese mother or something similar. It showed in his colouring, but although Harriet didn't know it his height and breadth came from a Texan father. The combination was, as Ella had said, quite breathtaking.

'Nice to meet you, Harriet,' he said warmly, and his fingers closed around hers for a moment in a gesture that was almost a caress. Startled she raised her eyes to his and saw that he was watching her closely. She quickly withdrew her hand and without realising it took a step away from him. Lewis's mouth curved in a smile.

'Rowena and I hope you'll be happy here,' he continued smoothly. 'I'm afraid life can be a bit chaotic, but she tells me you're tired of routine work so that shouldn't worry you.'

'It will certainly be different,' responded Harriet, wishing that she wasn't quite so aware of his physical presence. She was busy admiring the breadth of his shoulders compared to his slim hips, and that wasn't the way she usually responded to men. What made it worse was that he seemed to know because he hardly took his gaze off her.

'Is Chris around, darling?' asked Lewis, draping an arm casually around Rowena's shoulders.

Rowena smiled up at him. 'I think I saw him coming back from the pool.'

'Give him a call, then Harriet will know the three most important people in the house!' He laughed, but softly, as though at some private joke.

Rowena left the room for a moment and Harriet decided that she wasn't going to stand around feeling like an awkward schoolgirl, so she sat down on the low sofa and immediately watched her hemline rise to her thighs again.

Lewis glanced briefly at her legs and then away. Harriet wondered if he was simply so used to seeing women's legs that they no longer interested him, or if Rowena's were far better than hers. For some ridiculous reason she hoped it wasn't the latter. She'd always thought her legs were one of her best points.

'I hope you and Rowena get along all right,' said Lewis quietly. 'She's going through a difficult time at the moment. The film we're getting ready is going to test her like she's never been tested before. She needs a lot of understanding and support. Sometimes she can seem difficult, but it's insecurity. You find most actors and actresses are basically insecure.'

'I'd be insecure if my work depended on my appearance,' said Harriet.

Lewis looked directly at her. 'I don't think you'd have any reason for your insecurity.'

Harriet went warm at the unexpected compliment and couldn't think how to respond. 'I think Rowena's beautiful,' she said eventually.

'She was beautiful, but at thirty the camera can be very unkind.'

'Is she thirty? She doesn't look it!' exclaimed Harriet.

Lewis raised an eyebrow. 'You're learning fast. That's exactly the kind of thing she needs to hear.'

'But it's true,' protested Harriet.

'Having you here won't help her believe that,' he remarked.

'Well, she chose me. It isn't my fault I'm only twenty-three.'

'Of course not,' said Lewis reassuringly, knowing that it was he and not Rowena who'd chosen Harriet, and his choice had been a very careful one. He needed to stoke Rowena's insecurity, to trigger off some form of jealousy if the plan was to work. It was the only way he could think of to help her.

An awkward silence fell, but then the door opened and Rowena returned with a slim, blond-haired, blue-eyed young man behind her. His complexion was fresh and at first glance he looked little more than a boy, but on closer inspection Harriet thought he was probably in his late twenties.

'Chris, this is Harriet Radcliffe,' said Rowena proudly. 'Harriet, I'd like you to meet Chris Falkener, my half-brother.'

Harriet sat forward on the sofa and shook hands

with the young man who was staring at her quite openly. 'You're a knock-out!' he exclaimed in apparent surprise. 'Whatever were you thinking of, Rowena, letting a beautiful young lady like this loose in the house?'

To Harriet's dismay Rowena flushed and in the light from the window it looked as though there were tears in her eyes, although when she spoke her voice was quite steady. 'Don't be silly, Chris, you'll embarrass Harriet. Besides, why shouldn't I have an attractive personal assistant for a change? You know I like beautiful things around me.'

'Things yeah, but not women. Well, you're the nicest surprise I've had since Christmas, Harriet. Welcome to our little family.'

Harriet smiled politely, but her first impression of him wasn't favourable. He seemed spoilt and ill-mannered, and it was difficult to believe he was Rowena's half-brother.

After the introductions a maid was summoned to take Harriet to her rooms. 'If there's anything you don't like, let me know,' said Rowena with a smile. 'We want you to feel really at home here. Part of the family unit.'

'Thank you,' said Harriet politely, privately thinking that as a personal assistant she was unlikely to be involved in their domestic life, and in any case it was hardly a family. A husband, wife and half-brother didn't seem to her to symbolise a close-knit unit, exclusion from which would be devastating. She decided it was just a typical exaggeration by an actress.

Her rooms astonished her. She had expected them to be large, but not particularly plush. In fact the bedroom, decorated in varying shades of blue, looked large enough for two couples rather than a single female. The deep blue carpet flecked with white was wool, its pile thick and luxurious beneath her feet, and was beautifully complemented by the blue curtains patterned with tiny white flowers. As for the bed, Harriet could hardly believe her eyes at the sight of it.

It was enormous, the largest bed she'd ever seen, and at each corner an ornate gold column rose up at least five feet towards the ceiling, while at the foot of the bed the gold theme was continued with a twisted rope pattern that led from each of the side poles to meet in the middle in a two-feet-tall figure of two lovers embracing. The blue and white padded headboard was unusually high and surrounded by a design that matched the entwined gold rope at the opposite end.

The en suite bathroom was a total contrast. The

floor was covered in white rugs and the bath was white enamel set in a solid wood surround and shaped to fit the body, broad at one end, then narrowing at the end where the taps were. It was also unexpectedly deep, and Harriet wondered if there was enough hot water for everyone in the house to fill similar baths.

On the walls were tiny pen and ink etchings, all framed in wood that matched the bath surround. On closer inspection Harriet could see that each etching showed a couple engaged in some form of love-making, most of them the kind of positions that made her ache at the very prospect.

At her bedside table was a telephone, and on a sudden impulse she picked it up and dialled Ella's number. For once it wasn't the answerphone and Ella was clearly delighted to hear from her.

As soon as Harriet lifted her receiver a light flashed on the phone in Lewis's study and he carefully picked up his own handset, then sat listening with interest to Harriet's conversation.

'Ella, you were right!' she said dramatically.

'About what?' asked Ella, intrigued by Harriet's unusual enthusiasm.

'Rowena's husband. He is incredibly handsome, and

there's something about him I can't explain it but it just makes you feel weird all over when he looks at you.'

'Nice weird?'

'Of course! I know now that I was right to leave James. I never once lusted after him in all the years I knew him!'

'You mean you lust after Lewis James? Harriet, he's a respectable married man!' laughed Ella.

'I know, disgraceful isn't it? I can't help it, Ella. I'd give anything to know what it was like to have a man like that make love to me. Still, I'll settle for living in the same house.'

'I wouldn't,' said Ella bluntly, and in his study Lewis smiled. 'You should go for it,' continued Ella. 'It could be difficult though, he's not what you'd call a ladies' man. As far as I know from the gossip columns he's been faithful to Rowena Farmer since they married, and word has it that even she comes second to his work.'

'Sounds quite a challenge,' said Harriet.

'Let me know if you make any progress!' laughed Ella. 'What are your rooms like?'

'I've only seen my bedroom and bathroom, and they're out of this world. I'm sure the living-room will be just as grand.'

'Better than working for Mr Grant, I take it?' queried Ella.

'No comparison!' agreed Harriet. 'I'd better go now. Oh yes, one thing. Did you know Rowena Farmer had a half-brother called Chris?'

Ella hesitated. 'Now you come to mention it I did read something about him once. I think he only gets to act in her films, you know – a kind of hanger-on. Why, is he there too?'

'Yes, but he doesn't look anything like her. In fact, I wasn't that struck on him.'

'That's because you only had eyes for Lewis,' laughed Ella. 'I'll have to go now. I'm auditioning in half an hour, but keep me up to date, won't you?'

'I certainly will,' Harriet assured her and when she replaced the receiver she failed to notice the faint click as Lewis did the same.

Her living-room was equally luxurious, the colour theme an unusual burnt orange with cream furniture, including an antique chaise longue and the largest arm-chair Harriet had ever seen.

When she went back into her bedroom the maid was unpacking her clothes and hanging them in the cup-boards. 'Miss Farmer would like to see you downstairs in the conservatory when you're ready,' she informed Harriet.

'I'll go now,' Harriet said quickly. 'Where is it?'

'Just past the bottom of the staircase, first door on your left.'

When Harriet entered Rowena was sitting slumped in a wicker chair, her head back and her face drained of its usual colour. Harriet cleared her throat and at once the film star's head came up and a professional sparkle returned to her features.

'Was everything all right, Harriet?' she asked sweetly.

'The rooms are incredible; I shall get thoroughly spoilt here.'

'I hope so,' said Rowena vaguely. 'You must help me get this room straight. It needs lots of potted plants, spice ropes – that kind of thing. Would you see to it for me?'

Harriet, though she thought the clean uncluttered lines of the room very attractive, agreed. If Rowena wanted plants, plants it should be.

Harriet stood by the large glass windows of the conservatory and stared out across the grass that gently sloped away from the back of the house.

'I hadn't realised quite how beautiful you were,' said Rowena suddenly.

Harriet turned to look at her. 'I'm sorry?'

'You're young as well.'

'I'm twenty-three,' said Harriet, wondering why Rowena should suddenly start talking about her PA's appearance.

'Unfortunately I'm not. I hadn't expected Chris to find you so attractive.' Harriet, uncertain as to what she should say, kept silent. 'Did you find him attractive?' continued Rowena.

Harriet gave a small smile, embarrassed by the question. 'I really don't know – I hardly saw him-but not especially. He isn't my type.'

'Then what is your "type", as you so quaintly put it?' queried Rowena.

Now Harriet realised that she was in trouble. 'I prefer dark men,' she said slowly.

'Then presumably you find my husband attractive, if not my half-brother?'

Harriet wished Rowena would change the subject. If she kept on like this it was going to be impossible not to antagonise her, and her voice already had an edge to it, as though she was annoyed by something Harriet had done.

'He's very handsome,' she replied diplomatically.

'Handsome! Yes, of course he's handsome, but so are thousands of men. Isn't he attractive to you?'

'I hadn't thought about it,' lied Harriet.

Rowena sat up straight in her chair. 'That's a lie. I saw the way you looked at him. You felt it, the same as all women do. You wanted him, didn't you? Even then, in those first moments, you were wondering what it would be like to go to bed with him.'

'I most certainly was not!' said Harriet, trying her best to sound offended. 'I'm sorry, Rowena, but I'm not sure where this is leading. Have I done something wrong? Would you like me to leave, is that it?'

Rowena leant across the table towards her. 'I think perhaps there's something you should know,' she said slowly.

'And what could that be?' asked Lewis, strolling into the room and pouring himself a mug of coffee from the percolator on the table.

Rowena turned her head towards him. 'I didn't hear you coming, darling.'

He smiled at her, and absentmindedly ran the fingers of his left hand down her bare arm. Rowena stretched and made a small sound of pleasure. His arm slid up to her shoulder and pushed the mass of red-gold hair behind her ear so that he could softly stroke the side of her neck. 'What did you want Harriet to know?' he repeated.

'I can't remember now, you've distracted me!' laughed Rowena. 'It wasn't important, only something about my fan mail.'

Lewis looked over at Harriet. 'My wife gets a lot of fan mail. You'll spend a great deal of time answering it, I'm afraid. She has ten standard letters of reply on the computer, all designed to appear personal. You just have to be careful to check that the person you're replying to hasn't written before. If they have then the letter's on a separate disk and you choose from ten follow-up replies. "How wonderful to hear from you again", that kind of thing.'

'Do people write more than once?' asked Harriet.

'Darling, sometimes they write every week,' laughed Rowena. 'The only difference then is that we call them cranks, not fans, and bin the letters.'

'Haven't you ever had a crush on a film star?' asked Lewis.

Harriet shook her head. 'I'm not very well up on films, or plays for that matter. I like museums, art galleries and antique shops, but not acting.'

'You'll be good for us then. We're usually surrounded by people bitten by the acting bug.' He looked
thoughtfully at her. 'I imagine you're too sensible to let
your heart get the better of your head in any situation.'

He made the remark sound like an insult. 'I prefer to
keep my emotions hidden,' said Harriet coolly. 'Now,
perhaps there are some things I could do for you, Miss
Farmer.'

'Please, not Miss Farmer,' laughed Rowena, suddenly
relaxed and friendly again. 'You must always call me
Rowena. I'm sure we're going to be friends.'

Harriet wasn't sure about anything any more, except
for the fact that watching Lewis's hands stray over
Rowena's arm and neck had been highly unsettling and
left her face feeling hot. 'I'm sorry, Rowena it is. What
would you like me to do?'

'The fan mail then, if you're desperate to start earn-
ing your keep. Lewis, be an angel and show her the
room where she'll be working. I simply must have
another cup of coffee.'

'Sure.' Lewis put his own mug down and led Harriet
up the open staircase and through a door on the first
floor. 'We've earmarked this for your office. The computer, telephone and fax machine are all in place, but

although we've got the filing cabinets in I'm afraid none of Rowena's correspondence has been put away. We thought you'd like to use your own system.'

Harriet stared about the room. It was light and airy, the furniture all solid mahogany and the walls covered in heavy patterned wallpaper. 'It's certainly big enough!' she said with a smile.

'All the rooms are large. This seemed the best because Rowena has a room through the adjoining door there where she goes to learn her lines, try on clothes, experiment with make-up – that kind of thing. It means you'll be near when she might need you.'

'Fine. So where are the fan letters?' asked Harriet, standing facing the desk and looking over the piles of papers set out on it.

Lewis came up behind her and she felt his body brush against her back as he reached over her shoulder. 'I think they're there,' he said quietly.

Harriet straightened slightly and her buttocks and thighs pressed up against him. She half-turned in order to move away but her arm caught the pile of papers at the end of the desk and it went flying. As she bent down to pick them up, Lewis bent as well and their hands met as they reached in unison for one of the letters.

Again, just as at their first meeting, Lewis's fingers seemed to linger on hers. This time the pads of his fingertips brushed along the tops of her fingers and she shivered suddenly. Slowly her stood up, letting his hand trail up her arm and over her shoulder before removing it.

'I'll leave you to sort them out then,' he said calmly.

Harriet nodded, her mouth so dry she wasn't sure she'd be able to speak. It had been deliberate, she was certain of that; his touch, the way his body had moved against hers had indicated that. Yet in his eyes and voice there was no sign of interest or desire. Perhaps he was just very tactile, she told herself as he left the room.

After leaving Harriet, Lewis went in search of Rowena. He found her sitting on the tiles by the side of the large, heated indoor pool, her arms wrapped round her knees. For a moment he looked down at her thoughtfully, well aware of the kind of thoughts that must be going through her head at the moment, then he pulled one of the loungers forward and sat down on it.

'As I thought, she's perfect,' he said casually.

Rowena turned to look at him. 'I didn't expect Chris to be so impressed,' she said miserably.

'Of course he was impressed. I knew he would be; that was one of the main considerations in choosing her. That and her youth,' he added thoughtfully.

Rowena flushed. 'Chris is older than I am.' Her tone was defensive.

'Only by eighteen months! In any case, the older men get, the younger the women they desire.'

'Stop doing this!' shouted Rowena, standing up and glaring down at him. 'You of all people know how much I worry about my age. I expect Chris to be cruel, but not you.'

'Then why do you love Chris more?' asked Lewis softly.

The anger faded from Rowena's eyes and a look of despair filled them. 'I don't know! I wish I did. I wish I could tear myself away from him, but I can't. He's like a drug. Even when I think I'm getting free he draws me back.'

'Which is precisely why we're making this film, remember?'

'I don't think I can go through with it.'

Lewis frowned. 'Nonsense. In any case, you have no

choice. No one else is anxious to put you in a film. I'm your only hope.'

'But why this film, this story?'

He sighed. They'd been over it so many times and still she seemed unable, or unwilling, to understand. 'Rowena, I've never done fiction before. My films have all had social messages, or exposed corruption. When this idea was put to me I didn't want to do it either. I was afraid, just as you're afraid now. But then I realised how perfect it was for us. A film about a brother and sister whose sexual relationship began when they were in their teens and refused to die. A man who marries the sister, knowing all about the relationship but thinking he can take her away from her brother, only to find that he can't. It's *our* story, it isn't fiction; it's our problem and if it's our problem it's other people's problem too. No one knows because it isn't something people talk about. AIDS yes, or drug addiction or alcoholism, but not sibling incest. This might help people, but more importantly it might help us.'

She stared at him. 'There was no other woman in that original idea you were sent.'

Lewis smiled. 'But it needed a catalyst. Someone who would force all the others to reassess their lives, make decisions instead of letting the situation drift. Once I'd thought of that I knew it could be a special film; all I needed to do was see the drama played out for real first, to make sure that I got it right. That's why the scriptwriters are here in England. I'll have regular meetings with them, tell them what direction the story takes every step of the way. We *are* the film, Rowena, and then when it's over you'll star in the screen version and you'll have all your emotional recall to use. Believe me, with the film done this way you could end up with an Oscar.'

As he'd known it would the very word made Rowena's eyes brighten, but then she frowned again. 'What if I don't like the ending?'

He tried hard to keep any hint of irritation out of his voice. 'It doesn't matter if you like it or not; it will be truthful, and that's what I want, a truthful film about a forbidden subject.'

Rowena ran her hands through her hair, sweeping it back behind her ears, and turned towards the pool again, revealing her famously perfect profile. 'You're using me,' she said sullenly. 'I don't believe you love me or you wouldn't do this.'

'If you loved me, you'd leave your half-brother,'

Lewis's voice was soft, but she could hear the annoyance beneath.

'Perhaps if I'd felt safer with you I would have left him,' she responded.

Lewis stood up, unable to control his temper any longer. 'If you remember, Rowena, it was you who came to me in hysterical tears begging me to help you. I've never interfered, never tried to come between you and Chris. I knew about him when we married and I accepted him. All the dramas, all the weeping and wailing have come from you. And not only do you claim you want to be rid of him, you also want "to be a proper actress". Well, for your information real acting hurts. You have to put yourself through a hell of a lot of emotional pain if you're going to pull off a part like this. I warned you before we began, but you said it was what you wanted. I'm afraid there's too much money involved for you to pull out now.'

Rowena turned and pressed herself against her husband's body. 'Make love to me,' she whispered.

'No,' said Lewis, gently removing her arms from around his neck.

Startled she took a step backward. 'Why not?'

'I haven't time right now.'

'You've always had time before.'

He kissed her gently on the mouth. 'Then perhaps I just don't want to,' he murmured, and to her dismay he walked away, back into the house.

Chapter Three

HARRIET HAD BEEN working for Rowena for a
week now and she still didn't understand her.
Sometimes she was charm itself, smiling, making jokes
and sharing female confidences with Harriet as though
they were friends. At other times she was sullen and
withdrawn, criticising everything Harriet did and
impossible to please.

It didn't worry Harriet. She accepted it as part of
Rowena's artistic temperament, and even if it had worried her, being near Lewis would have been ample
compensation. With every day that passed she found
herself more and more obsessed by him. She was sure
that he was interested in her. Whenever Rowena had

been particularly difficult he would go out of his way to be extra warm towards Harriet, as though he knew exactly the kind of day she'd had. He was always watching her too, yet he still was clearly in love with his wife, forever touching or stroking her as he passed.

Once Harriet had come upon them embracing passionately on the stairs. Lewis's back had been to the wall and Rowena's legs were straddling his right thigh as she pressed her body against his. Although Harriet had retreated as quietly as possible the image had stayed with her and seemed to return almost every night when she was trying to get to sleep.

On this particular day she'd been working on the computer nearly non-stop for the entire morning and when she straightened up for lunch her neck and shoulders were rigid with tension. Rowena came in to sign the fan mail and looked at her sympathetically.

'You've spent too long hunched over that machine. Why don't you have a massage? My masseur's in the house somewhere – you're welcome to use her.'

Harriet couldn't think of anything nicer. 'That would be great. Are you having lunch today?' she added. Rowena's eating habits were unpredictable.

Rowena shook her head. 'Tell Lewis I'm going over

something with Chris, would you? There's a script he's been sent to look at. He needs my advice.'

'Of course,' agreed Harriet. Privately she thought it highly unlikely that Chris would ever be anything like the kind of star his half-sister was, but she'd already come to realise that in Rowena's eyes Chris was perfect.

They always had lunch in the spacious conservatory, although it was no longer quite so spacious since Harriet had obeyed Rowena's instructions and half-filled it with exotic green plants, which the film star herself attended to every day, claiming it was therapeutic for her.

Lewis looked up when Harriet entered. 'No Rowena?'

'She and Chris have a script to go through.'

He looked surprised. 'Really? I'm surprised she didn't mention it to me. Did it come through the post today?'

'If it did, I didn't open it,' replied Harriet. 'Do you know where Rowena's masseur is?' she added. 'My shoulders are stiff and she said I could use her.'

'She's gone I'm afraid, but I'm very good at reflexology. Would that help?' Harriet assumed he was joking and smiled politely. 'I'm serious,' he continued. 'Rowena finds it very helpful. Why not try it?'

Harriet's heart seemed to jump in her chest as she thought about Lewis using his hands on her, letting his long slim fingers massage her feet. She longed for it, but for some reason the words of acceptance refused to pass he rlips.

'Come along,' said Lewis briskly. 'Sit in the basket chair by the window and I'll do it before we eat.'

He sounded so matter-of-fact that some of her awk-wardness faded. Even if her thoughts were running along sexual lines it didn't seem as if his were, and this chastening realisation made it easier for her to do as he said.

She sat in the chair and slipped off her high heeled shoes. 'What about your stockings?' he asked with a smile.

'I wear tights,' said Harriet, realising this was hardly a sexy admission.

Lewis pulled a face. 'How dull! Well, I can't massage your feet through tights; you'll have to slip them off.'

Harriet went to go into another room but he blocked her way. 'For heaven's sake, Harriet, I've seen more actresses changing clothes than you've typed letters!'

'Sorry,' she mumbled and her hands slid up beneath her thankfully full skirt and she tugged her tights down in what she was aware was a decidedly unerotic display of stripping.

'Now sit down and relax,' Lewis commanded her, but Harriet's shoulders felt worse than when she'd finished working for Rowena. She watched as Lewis took a bottle of olive oil from the work top then sat on the wooden floor at her feet, his legs tucked sideways. He drew her right foot on to the top of his thighs, poured some of the oil into the palm of one hand, rubbed his hands together and slowly, with firm but gentle kneading movements, worked his way from the centre of the her foot towards the sides. He began at the heel and in a leisurely fashion moved towards the toes. When he reached the soft padded part of the sole behind the toes themselves he pushed his thumb down hard and rotated it in tiny circles.

As he worked Harriet could feel her whole body responding. Her shoulders and neck muscles did relax but the rest of her didn't. She could feel her breathing quickening and her nipples brushing against her silk camisole top.

It was as much as she could do stop herself from

wriggling around on the seat of the cushioned wicker chair, and when Lewis glanced up at her face she felt sure that he must know from her face exactly the effect he was having on her.

Lewis did. He reached for the oil again and dipped a forefinger into it before softly pushing his slippery digit in and out between each of Harriet's toes in turn, twisting it from side to side as he went. The sexual implication behind the movement, coupled with the marvellously erotic sensation, made Harriet feel as though she was turning into liquid and she knew she was becoming moist between her thighs.

When he'd finished with her right foot he put it tenderly to the floor and proceeded to repeat the whole process with her left. It was almost more than she could bear; the tender, sensual caresses that soothed and yet aroused at the same time made her whole body long for his touch. If he could have this much effect on her by touching her feet she wondered what would happen if he moved on to more intimate places.

As he reached her toes for the second time and his silken finger slipped insinuatingly between them she suddenly felt her thighs begin to tremble and the whole of her lower body tightened. To her shock and horror she realised that if he didn't stop she was going to have an orgasm, and she tried to draw her foot away.

'Keep still,' he whispered. 'Let yourself relax. Enjoy it, that's the whole idea.'

'No, really I'm fine now I ...'

It was too late and before she could finish her sentence Harriet's body was shaken by a tiny tremor and her toes curled upwards with the pleasure. She was mortified, but if Lewis knew what had happened he gave no sign of it. He merely ran his hands over the arch of her foot in one final tender caress and then took her foot off his thigh.

'Better?' he asked politely.

Harriet, her face flushed and her pupils dilated, managed to nod and mutter a strangled, 'Yes, much better thank you.'

'Then you'd better put your tights back on, unless you prefer to be without them? It's a shame to cover your legs. I like long, bare, tanned legs – very sexy indeed.'

Still in a daze, Harriet muttered something about tanning easily and stumbled to her seat at the table. Lewis sat opposite her and broke off a piece of French bread then passed her Parma ham and cheese.

Her hands still trembling slightly, Harriet began to eat. When Lewis poured her a glass of wine without asking she didn't comment, although normally she never drank at lunch-time because it made her too sleepy to work in the afternoon. Today she felt she needed it.

'How are you enjoying working here?' he enquired casually.

'Very much; it's certainly not boring.'

'No, I imagine not. But what about your social life? You haven't had a day off yet. When were you planning on taking some time for yourself?'

'I thought I'd probably go and spend the weekend at my flat if I'm not needed,' said Harriet. 'Rowena said you were entertaining on Saturday night, so I thought I'd be better out of the way and in any case I've promised to meet a friend soon.'

'A male friend?' asked Lewis, his eyes smiling at her in what was very definitely an intimate manner.

Harriet shook her head. 'No, a girlfriend.'

'Tell me, what was your last lover like?' he asked politely.

The wine she was drinking went down the wrong way, and Harriet was shaken by a coughing fit. He was obviously trying to shock her, she thought to herself as she began to recover. Well, he wasn't going to succeed. He might be handsome and sensual but she wasn't prepared to let him make a fool of her.

'Adequate,' she said levelly when she could speak again.

'Adequate!' What a very good description. I can almost picture him from that one word. And the one before him?'

'Inadequate. I'm afraid there's only one before that, and he was even worse so this conversation isn't going to be very interesting,' said Harriet.

'At least they've got progressively better,' he laughed.

'Perhaps it's just that I've improved,' said Harriet, astonished at her own boldness.

'There's always that possibility, of course, but the right partner can make a very big difference.'

Considering that he'd just brought her to a climax by massaging her feet, this was scarcely news to Harriet. She couldn't help thinking about the number of times she'd laboured for what seemed an eternity in order to achieve any kind of satisfaction with James.

'I'd like to make love to you,' he said softly.

'I'm sure you say that to every woman you meet,' responded a startled Harriet.

'No, I don't. In fact, I'm very fussy.'

'Then I'm flattered.'

He reached across the table and gripped her by both wrists. 'You want me too, don't you?'

The way her flesh was responding now, let alone earlier, it would have been stupid to say no, thought Harriet, but she still had enough control of herself to remember why she was in this house in the first place.

'Even if I do, you're married to Rowena,' she reminded him.

He let his fingers stroke the exquisitely soft flesh of her inner wrists. 'We have a very open marriage. Believe me, Rowena wouldn't mind in the least.'

'Perhaps I mind.'

He moved one hand to stroke the side of her face. 'That would be rather a waste, don't you think?'

Harriet swallowed hard. The wine had dulled her brain, and his insistent touching of her, although only on her wrists and face, was proving irresistible. 'Please, don't do this,' she said quietly. 'I like my work. It will make things too awkward. I'd have to go and—'

Lewis stood up and moved swiftly round the table to stand next to her. Then he drew her to her feet and tipped her chin up so that she was looking directly into his eyes. 'I promise you, your work won't be affected. Trust me, I know what I'm doing. I don't want you to leave any more than you do. That won't be a problem.'

All the time he was speaking he was touching her. His hands were moving through her hair, smoothing her forehead, gentling her until she was leaning against him, her head on his chest, and she could feel his arousal clearly through his linen trousers.

'Take this afternoon off,' he whispered in her ear. 'Rowena's busy, you've worked all the morning, no one will mind. I want to make love to all of you, not just your feet. I want to touch you everywhere, to drive you mad with pleasure. Please, Harriet, let me do that.'

Every word, every touch inflamed Harriet's already clamouring senses until she knew that she was going to give in. It was what she'd wanted ever since she set eyes on him, and whatever the result she knew it would be worth it.

'I'd like that,' she said huskily.

Without another word Lewis took her hand and led her up two flights of stairs to the second floor, where she'd never been before. There he drew her into his bedroom, closing and locking the bedroom door behind him to ensure total privacy.

For a moment, as she saw the enormous bed, the piles of pillows and his discarded clothes scattered around the room, Harriet hesitated. This was a man more experienced than she could ever hope to be, a man who'd had countless women and would probably expect far more from her than she'd be able to give.

'What is it? What's the matter?' he murmured, sensing her fear.

'I'm afraid I'll disappoint you,' she said quietly.

'You couldn't,' he assured her. 'We'll be perfect together, as long as you trust me. You do trust me, don't you?'

Harriet nodded.

Watching from the adjoining room through a cleverly concealed peephole, Chris gave a smothered laugh and turned to his half-sister. 'She trusts Lewis!' he exclaimed. 'Talk about an innocent. Aren't you going to watch?'

Rowena, who had a comfortable seat by another spyhole, nodded. 'Of course, but I can't be bothered with his chat-up lines. Tell me when the action starts.'

'It's starting,' murmured Chris. 'He's about to undress her.'

Totally unaware of the hidden watchers, Harriet felt Lewis's hands unfastening the waistband of her skirt and as it fell to the floor she stepped out of it, grateful for the fact that she hadn't, in the end, bothered to replace her tights earlier. She knew that her long legs were shown to advantage by the angled cut-away tops of her cream-coloured french knickers but was less certain as to how he would respond to the rest of her body.

With infinite slowness, Lewis unbuttoned her blouse, peeling it back to expose the cream-coloured camisole top beneath. She wasn't wearing a bra and he drew one of the thin silken straps off her left shoulder, but to her surprise did not remove the garment.

'Keep it on,' he murmured, 'I prefer you like that.'

All the time he was undressing her his hands had moved up and down her legs, back and stomach and now, as he lowered her carefully on to the bed, he sat at her feet and nibbled lightly at her calves and the sensitive skin behind her knees.

Under his expert manipulation Harriet was encouraged to stretch out and give her body over to him. He

didn't seem to expect anything from her except acceptance. She saw him reach across to his bedside table and
pour something from a bottle into one hand, and the
next moment he was massaging jasmine-scented lotion
into her abdomen with the palm of his hand.

Harriet closed her eyes as the wonderful sensations
swept over her.

'No,' he said firmly. 'Look at me, I want to watch
your expressions change. I need to see what you like
and what you don't.'

She felt ridiculously shy letting him watch her; she'd
always closed her eyes with James, it had felt safer that
way. Lewis's words made it impossible for her to pretend she was alone, which was what she'd always done
before. He was forcing her to be more involved and this
added a new dimension of excitement.

The lotion was spread over her legs, including her
inner thighs, but when he came to her sex-lips he
simply brushed lightly over them, ignoring her sudden
upward-thrusting movement.

Next he worked his way over her rib cage, moving
the delicate lace camisole top back as he went until it
was rucked up over the top of her breasts, which were
now rapidly swelling, the blue veins becoming more

obvious as her excitement grew. Once more he ignored this erogenous zone and merely let the tips of his fingers dance across the surface before spreading the lotion over her shoulders and down the insides of her arms.

Every nerve in Harriet's body seemed to be alive now. She was trembling with excitement and frantic for more intimate touches but when she reached for his hand to try and move it where she wanted he shook his head. 'It's better to wait,' he assured her.

In the adjoining room Chris felt his own breathing quicken. Lewis was playing her with consummate skill, and her restlessly moving legs and upthrusting young breasts were testimony to her arousal. He himself was hard, and longed to be allowed to join in, to take the girl in the ways that he liked, the ways that kept Rowena enthralled. He was surprised by his reaction. Normally he would simply have wanted Rowena more than ever, but he knew that he was going to have to have Harriet before too long.

At last Lewis took pity on Harriet and lightly kneaded some of the lotion into each of her breasts in turn. He heard her breath catch in her throat and her eyes were grateful. Then, to Harriet's surprise, he moved himself up the bed so that he was straddling her body above the waist and, grasping his penis, he used the tip to trace a line around each nipple. The sensation was so glorious that Harriet reached up to increase the pressure on her nipples but again he restrained her, insisting on dictating the pace himself.

When she began to whimper softly with rising excitement he moved his body to the side of her and turned himself around so that he could spread the lotion on to her swelling vulva.

Harriet gasped at the first touch of his fingers on the delicate tissue, her hips moved without her knowledge and tight cords of sexual excitement seemed to connect her nipples to the core of her, where he was caressing her now, so that she couldn't tell where her pleasure was coming from. She only knew that her whole body was screaming with desire for release from the tight, mounting tension.

At last, when she was going frantic with desire, he let one of his fingers move slowly and delicately to the clitoris itself and massaged the side of the tiny swollen bud until her whimpers turned to moans and he could see her belly tightening and expanding as her whole pelvic area engorged with blood.

'Please,' whispered Harriet.

'Please what?' he teased, inserting two fingers inside her and rotating them just inside where he knew she would be most sensitive.

'Take me now,' she begged, and behind the peephole Chris fought almost as hard as Harriet to control himself while Rowena watched not the unfolding scene but her half-brother's face.

'Not yet,' he responded, feeling around the opening of her vagina for the tiny little bump that would show him where her G-spot was, while at the same time he continued to caress around her clitoris. 'And you mustn't come yet either.'

Harriet couldn't believe what he was saying. Her body was screaming for release, building towards what she felt certain would be the biggest orgasm she'd ever had and he was telling her not to come.

'I must,' she moaned. 'I can't help it.'

'Don't disappoint me, Harriet,' he murmured. 'It's better to delay the final moment.'

'Then stop touching me like that!' she cried, 'I can't bear it.'

'Of course you can. You can do anything I say,' he assured her, and his fingers kept up their skilful manipulations as Harriet's body seemed to swell and bunch in its frantic climb to the peak of ecstasy.

She bit on her lower lip, tried to think of other things, to ignore what his fingers were doing, but it was impossible. Her whole body was damp and hot with need and there was an ache above her pubic bone that was increasing every time he touched her.

Suddenly Lewis found the elusive G-spot. He flicked his finger back and forth across it while the hand that was on her vulva grasped the hard damp clitoris between two fingers and squeezed with almost imperceptible pressure.

He knew it would finish her, but still murmured, 'Not yet.'

Harriet heard the words but her body took over. With a scream that was almost one of pain so intense were the feelings, she gave herself up to the forbidden pleasure and her back arched up off the bed as the glorious rippling contractions tore through her in what seemed like an endless spasm of bliss until at last she was finished and fell back limply on to the bed.

'That was nearly very good,' said Lewis tenderly.

Harriet couldn't imagine how it could get any better. She looked at him through half-closed eyes and saw that his erection was enormous, far larger than that of any of her previous lovers, and the purple glans had a glistening drop of clear liquid at the end. His obvious need for her acted as an aphrodisiac and she reached out for him.

'Turn over,' he murmured. 'Put your face down on the pillow and bend your legs up from the knees.' She obeyed without question, knowing that whatever he decided to do, however he took her, it would be wonderful.

Once she was in position, Lewis knelt upright between her knees and his large hands reached beneath her so that he could caress her lower stomach while his penis nudged the cheeks of her bottom apart.

Then, as his fingers caressed her increasingly slippery clitoris his erection slid along her equally damp channel and came to a halt at the entrance to her vagina. The sensations his fingers were causing had already started Harriet's body on another climb towards orgasm and when she felt the soft velvet of his flesh against her opening she thrust backwards to try and hurry him into her. She wanted the sensation of fullness, needed to feel him deep within her, taking as well as giving pleasure.

Lewis drew back a little, aware that sometimes he was too large for his partner's comfort unless she was thoroughly aroused but when Harriet continued to move restlessly against him he slowly let himself slide into her.

For Harriet there was a moment of discomfort as her body stretched to accommodate him, but then one of his fingers tapped lightly at the base of her clitoris and incredible sensations of melting pleasure spread through her lower body and with them came increased lubrication that made his movements within her easier.

Lewis was finding his own rhythm now, different from the one that he used on Rowena, who liked him to thrust hard and fast. This time he moved slowly, sliding in and out at a leisurely pace, pausing now and again to rotate his hips so that Harriet could feel him touching her vaginal walls in what was almost a massaging motion.

The tingling darts that preceded her orgasms began in earnest now, shooting up through her belly, and her breasts ached with need so that she wriggled on the bed, stimulating her nipples herself. She could hear her own soft cries of mounting excitement and the way Lewis's breathing was also quickening.

All at once he changed pace and thrust fiercely forward, hitting the front of her vaginal wall exactly on her G-spot so that at the same time as his fingers teased her pulsating bud of pleasure on the outside, he was stimulating the crucial place within her.

The result was a sudden rush of sexual arousal that seemed to flood upwards from her feet and suffuse every nerve ending in her body with sensation. Her heart pounded and her belly tightened as she reached the brink of orgasm.

Lewis knew that he couldn't hold back any longer. The sight of her bent submissively in front of him, her slender long legs pressed against his, her smooth back and shoulders twisting in excitement all drove him to a fever pitch. When he felt the onset of his own release he moved his right hand and let the fingers dig softly into the flesh just above Harriet's pubic bone.

She climaxed seconds before him, and the rippling contractions of her inner walls around him were the trigger for his release too. He groaned and finally thrust as hard as he did with Rowena, determined to get the maximum pleasure from this moment.

Harriet could feel him shuddering above her but she was more aware of her own body and the incredible relief from the long, slow build-up of tension he had given her. No previous lover had ever given her such pleasure and she was startled by the realisation of her body's possible potential.

When Lewis was finally spent he gently straightened Harriet's legs and lay down next to her, turning her so that they could look into each other's eyes. He smiled and she smiled back at him, clearly as sated as he'd hoped.

'I told you it would be good,' he murmured, letting his hands run through her hair and noticing the difference in texture from Rowena's. Where hers was thick and curly, Harriet's was straight and much finer, but he liked the softness of it and the lack of hair lacquer which Rowena always used to excess.

'I'm sure everyone tells you this, but you really are beautiful,' he said with a smile, tracing a line down her nose and across the middle of her mouth.

'No one's ever told me that,' she replied with total honesty. 'Attractive yes, but never beautiful.'

'Well I think you're beautiful, and the camera would too.'

'Camera?' She felt a momentary stirring of unease.

'I'm a film director, remember? I always look at bone

structure and profiles. I try and see what the camera would see. It would adore you.'

'It adores Rowena,' Harriet pointed out.

'Everyone adores Rowena. She has a particular kind of beauty. Yours is different, but it's still beauty.'

'You don't have to say that, you know,' remarked Harriet, letting her hands wander down the golden brown skin of his muscular chest.

'I wouldn't, if it weren't true. You're also very good at sex!' he added with a laugh.

'You made me feel good,' said Harriet with tenderness, and in the next room Chris nearly laughed aloud. He had to hand it to Lewis. He knew how to handle women, especially in the early stages of an affair, although he hadn't expected him to sound quite so enthusiastic.

Next to him Rowena turned away from the scene. 'He really likes her,' she said shortly, and walked out of the room.

When Harriet entered the dining-room at eight that evening and saw Lewis standing by the fireplace with his arm round Rowena she felt an immediate surge of jealousy. Only a few hours earlier his arms had been round her, in the most passionate sexual encounter of her life so far. Now, in front of her eyes, he was engaged in an open display of affection with another woman, and it hurt. The fact that this woman was his wife and Harriet the interloper didn't make it any easier.

Rowena smiled at her, but to Harriet's overactive imagination the smile seemed strained. 'You're looking very well tonight, Harriet. Taking the afternoon off obviously agreed with you.'

'I told Rowena you'd taken off for a few hours,' said Lewis smoothly. 'She'd got so used to your efficiency she'd quite forgotten you'd been working non-stop for a week.'

'Where did you go?' asked Chris, sitting down at table with a large glass of whisky in his hand.

'I went shopping,' said Harriet, caught unawares.

'How nice. What did you buy?' enquired Rowena.

'Nothing, I just window-shopped.'

'I wish Rowena exercised such self-control!' laughed Lewis.

'Anyone can tell Harriet knows a lot about self-control,' said Chris softly. 'Do you ever let yourself go, Harriet?'

This apparently innocent question brought a blush to Harriet's cheeks as she remembered how abandoned she'd been with Lewis. 'Not in public,' she said shortly.

'Then we must get together in private,' responded Chris.

Rowena frowned at him and turned to Lewis. 'Shall we eat? I'm exhausted and need an early night.'

He rang the small bell set in the middle of the table. The maid responded promptly, as she always did, and Harriet was extremely thankful when the food was served. She knew it was ridiculous to worry, that Rowena couldn't possibly know that had happened between her and Lewis that afternoon, but there was a distinctly strained atmosphere in the room and all she wanted to do was get away from the three of them.

The meal began with asparagus soup, followed by prawns and salmon in a delicious mayonnaise sauce served with a green salad and new potatoes. After that they all had slices of the cook's superb *tarte citronne*, then finally cheese and biscuits and coffee.

As usual Lewis ate well, while Rowena merely picked at the main course, pushed her dessert aside after one mouthful and ignored the cheese and biscuits.

'No appetite?' asked Chris, smiling at his half-sister as though at some private joke.

'I've put on three pounds. I need to be careful,' responded Rowena, glaring at him.

Lewis looked surprised. 'I didn't think you'd put on weight, in fact quite the reverse.'

'I'm flattered you've had time to notice,' retorted Rowena sharply.

'That's not fair,' said Chris. 'You know how important this project is to Lewis. He's been working hard on it all day, haven't you, Lew?'

His brother-in-law looked directly at him, his eyes cool. 'What do you mean by that?'

'Just that you've been busy!'

'No busier than you, I imagine. Harriet told me you were going over a script with Rowena. Was it good?'

Chris shrugged. 'Not really. We've binned it.'

'Do let me look before it gets thrown away. I might know someone who could use it.'

'I shredded it,' said Rowena.

'Goodness, it must have been bad!' laughed Lewis.

Harriet kept her eyes on her plate. She knew now that she wasn't mistaken. The other three were definitely sniping at each other beneath the cover of normal conversation and her own guilty conscience made the situation even worse.

'What shops did you wander round?' demanded Rowena abruptly.

Harriet swallowed her last fragment of cheese. 'I . . . Bond Street.'

'You mean there's a shop called Bond Street? I must go there.'

'No, of course there isn't a shop. I meant I wandered up and down Bond Street.'

'Was it busy?'

'Bond Street's always busy,' said Harriet calmly, but her stomach was churning as Rowena's questions continued.

'I think Harriet's private life is her own affair, Rowena,' said Lewis suddenly. 'If you're really tired, darling, do you want to go up to bed now?'

Rowena nodded. 'I think I will. I'll take a pill and go straight to sleep. Perhaps you wouldn't mind sleeping in your own room tonight.'

Lewis nodded. 'As you like. I've got a lot to do before I go up, so that way I won't have to worry about disturbing you.'

Rowena stood up. She looked at Harriet and opened

her mouth to speak. 'Good night, Rowena,' said Lewis sharply. At the sound of his voice she turned her head towards him, met his warning glance and quickly left the room.

'Not a good day for her, I'm afraid,' said Chris with an apologetic look at Harriet. 'She found a grey hair this morning, that's enough to ruin her week!'

'She doesn't have to worry, she's still beautiful,' said Harriet. 'A friend of mine is an actress and she was saying that she'd never seen anyone with such a magical presence as Rowena in her first film.'

'Yes, but that was a few years ago now. She was only your age then; it's harder to maintain that glowing illusion as the years pass.'

'She was twenty-three when she made *A Lady Calls?*'

'That's right, isn't it, Lewis?'

'Something like that,' he agreed, leaning across the table to refill Harriet's wine glass and running his thumb over the top of her fingers as he did so. She swallowed hard, hoping that Chris hadn't noticed.

After a few minutes Chris yawned and pushed back his chair. 'I think I'll go up too. I'll probably sleep off the meal and then do a few laps of the pool. According to Rowena I don't get enough exercise.

'Don't drown,' murmured Lewis.

Chris smiled sweetly at him. 'I'll try not to give you that pleasure. Good night, Harriet. Sleep well.'

'What did he mean?' asked Harriet as the door closed behind him. 'Why would his death give you pleasure?'

'He thinks I disapprove of him because he lives off Rowena,' said Lewis shortly. 'The truth is, I scarcely think about him at all.'

'Rowena was in a bad mood tonight. She can't have guessed, can she?' asked Harriet anxiously.

'Not unless you told her! Don't feel so guilty, Harriet. You are entitled to some pleasure in life.'

'But not with her husband,' protested Harriet.

'Don't tell me you're going to say we can't do it again.'

'It's awkward. When I see you with Rowena I feel terrible.'

Lewis looked annoyed. 'You seem to have some very middle-class hang-ups about sex.'

'Unlike you I'm not artistic, which seems to be a blanket term for lack of morals,' retorted Harriet, sounding more annoyed than she was because she wanted nothing more than to have Lewis make love to her again.

'If you think my morals are bad then perhaps I'd better show you something that will take away your guilt,' he said slowly.

'Show me what?'

Lewis caught hold of her wrist and pulled her roughly to her feet. 'Come with me, Harriet. I'll show you something that will make our little entertainment this afternoon seem like a Sunday school outing.'

Harriet tried to pull away from him. 'Let me go, I don't want to see anything.'

'I think you'll want to see this,' he assured her, and despite her protests he drew her out of the room and up the winding staircase, back to the second floor.

Chapter Four

WHEN LEWIS LED Harriet into a tiny room two doors down the landing from his bedroom she thought first that she was in a cupboard, but as her eyes grew accustomed to the darkness she realised that it had originally been intended as a dressing room, although the adjoining door had now been filled in. There was little furniture there, only a high backed chair and a two-seater settee in front of a square window, which let in no light at all.

She turned to Lewis in bewilderment. 'What is this room?'

'Sit here next to me on the sofa and look carefully at the window,' he said softly.

Puzzled, she stared at the glass, and after a few seconds realised that she was looking into a distinctly feminine bedroom lavishly decorated in various shades of lilac. As she watched, a figure crossed her line of vision, and she saw Rowena walking totally naked from her adjoining bathroom back to her bed.

Harriet ducked down and Lewis laughed. 'She can't see you, it's a two-way mirror.'

'You mean, anyone can sit here and watch her without her knowing?'

'Yes. It's surprising what you get to see as well.'

A knot of excitement formed in Harriet's chest as Rowena turned so that she was facing the hidden spectators. Her figure was superb, her breasts high and full with large nipples and her waist tiny, curving out into softly rounded hips which gave her the traditional hour-glass figure of the sex symbol. Only her legs were less than perfect. They were shorter than Harriet had expected from her films, and the calves of her legs clearly defined.

'Can she hear us?' whispered Harriet.

'Only if we crash about. She can't hear us talking, but unfortunately we can't hear her talking either.'

Harriet couldn't think why this mattered since

Rowena was only getting ready for bed, but almost as soon as Lewis had finished speaking a second figure entered Rowena's bedroom and Harriet's eyes grew wide with astonishment as the film star made no attempt to cover herself when Chris strode across the carpet towards her.

In the bedroom, totally unaware of what Lewis was doing, Rowena looked at her half-brother with a mixture of fear and longing. 'Not tonight, Chris,' she said softly. 'I really am tired and ...'

'You're not tired, you're afraid,' said Chris. 'Now that Lewis's little piece of *cinema verite* is underway you don't like it, do you?'

'How would you like seeing your wife making love to another man?' demanded Rowena.

'A stupid question since I don't have a wife and never intend to take one. I only need you, and you only need me, but you were too stupid to realise it. Perhaps this game of Lewis's will show you that at last.'

'I love Lewis,' protested Rowena.

'No, you love me,' said Chris fiercely. 'Lewis gives you respectability, and you think he's going to save your career, but you don't love him. He can't give you what I can, what you need, can he?'

'Leave it, Chris,' said Rowena, turning away. 'I need to sleep.'

'I need you,' he muttered and before she realised what was happening he'd grabbed her by the shoulders, pulled her arms behind her and tied them with a silk cord. She backed away towards the bed, already aroused, already longing for whatever he was going to do to her. 'I meant it,' she protested, 'I don't want you.'

Chris flicked at one of her erect nipples. 'This tells me a different story. I want you to wear the Japanese belt tonight.'

'No!' protested Rowena.

'You love it. Why deny yourself the pleasure?'

'Because you make it too intense.'

He smiled. 'Which is what you want, and why you need me so badly.' He reached into a drawer next to her bed and withdrew the slim rounded cord that fastened with a metal clip within which was a tiny spring. Very slowly Rowena moved towards him and when he fastened it around her she moistened her suddenly dry lips with the tip of her tongue. On the settee next to Harriet Lewis drew in his breath sharply at the look of naked sexuality on his wife's face.

'Now for the cloth,' murmured Chris.

Rowena stood at the foot of her bed, her hands still bound behind her as Chris fetched the long piece of silk material that went with the belt. He fastened it into the special openings in the belt at the back of her then drew it teasingly between her slightly opened thighs and up the front of her abdomen until he could fasten the other end in the front openings.

The cloth was now hanging loosely behind her thighs, but when Chris pressed on the side fastening of the belt the cloth was drawn upwards and he kept his finger there until it was brushing lightly against her vulva. He then released the spring. 'I think it's best to start with it loose, don't you?' he said reflectively.

Rowena shivered and he bent his head to tongue softly at the undersides of her famous breasts. 'I think I'll bind these too,' he whispered.

'No, please don't. Not both at the same time,' begged Rowena, but her words were all part of their game and Chris knew it. It was a game that had begun many years ago, when they'd first become aware of their bodies, and it had escalated out of control until now it sometimes didn't seem like a game to Rowena, but a contest of wills.

He licked and sucked at the still hardening nipples and when they were fully erect bound a silk scarf tightly round them, so that they could be seen straining against the cloth.

'Wonderful!' he enthused. 'Now we can begin.'

He guided Rowena backwards until she came to rest against the large chair on which she had earlier thrown her clothes. Sweeping these to the floor he lowered her on to it and then reclined the back. With her arms fastened behind her and her upper torso set at an angle this meant that her tightly bound breasts were even more prominent, and he pulled her lower in the chair until the cheeks of her bottom were balanced on the edge of the seat.

Unable to tear her eyes away from the scene that was unfolding in front of her, Harriet felt a stirring of sexual excitement in her own breasts and belly. She knew that she shouldn't be watching, that by doing so she was invading a very private and forbidden moment for Rowena, but even if Lewis hadn't had a restraining hand on her arm she knew that she wouldn't have left. She had to see what was to follow.

'Are you comfortable?' asked Chris.

Rowena nodded, wondering what his next move

would be and quivering with excited anticipation. It was always like this when they were together. Her body became alive in a way it never did for anyone else, not even Lewis no matter how skilfully he played with her body.

'I think I'd prefer you a little less comfortable,' mused Chris aloud, and reaching into his pocket he withdrew an object that Rowena knew only too well. It was a small vibrator with a bulbous head. She shook her head and pressed her bottom more firmly into the chair but Chris's hands easily lifted her and then he started to ease it into her back passage.

In the next room Harriet gasped and Lewis glanced at her. 'Haven't you ever tried that?'

She shook her head, wondering how Rowena could bear to take the object into such a tender part of her body.

Rowena was wondering the same thing, but as the walls of her rectum struggled to accommodate the vibrator, Chris crouched in front of her and lazily drew the tip of his tongue along the centre of the silk material covering her vulva. The feel of the warm dampness through the silk, the way the material then clung to her more tightly and her swelling clitoris all combined to make her twist her lower body with excitement and the twisting movement assisted Chris in his task until the head of the vibrator was finally drawn into her rectum and she felt it filling her until her bowels cramped with the pressure.

As soon as it was fully inserted Chris turned it on at the lowest setting, then pressed her into the seat so that she was left to endure the constant stimulation of her most sensitive nerve endings.

She writhed in an ecstasy of dark excitement and watched as he went across to the drinks cabinet and refrigerator that was always kept fully stocked in her bedroom. From the fridge he took ice-cubes, put them into the silver ice bucket and carried them over to Rowena.

She was making small whimpering sounds of excitement and he smiled as he carefully picked up one of the cubes with the tongs and then drew it in a straight line across both her breasts, making sure that her nipples and areolae received plenty of attention. He loved to see the dark outlines of the area appearing through the thin white material, and loved to watch Rowena's eyes as she was forced to wait for him to provide further stimulation. Without him she was helpless to gain her satisfaction, and he loved the feeling of power that this gave him, just as she adored the sensation of domination.

When her nipples were like two rigid peaks poking through the binding he nibbled at them with his teeth and she screamed with pleasure. 'Naughty!' he reproved her. 'You're going too fast.'

Rowena couldn't help it, her body's responses to him were shaming but uncontrollable.

'I'll have to punish you a little,' he said quictly, and pressed the button at the side of the Japanese belt. At once the material between her legs was drawn upwards and this time he didn't release the catch until it was tight against her sex-lips.

In her back passage the plug was still vibrating continuously and as the silky material pressed against her throbbing vulva the plug's pressure too was increased. Rowena's body trembled more violently and a tiny spasm of pleasure swept through her.

She gazed at Chris who gazed back at her, his eyes suddenly cold. 'Did you come then?' he asked his half-sister.

Rowena nodded.

'Tell me,' he ordered her.

'Yes, I came.' Her voice was dark with shame.

'You're losing control far too easily these days.' His tone was severe, and he reached beneath her to increase the speed of the vibrator. Once that was done he watched the titian-haired figure shuddering beneath the stimulation and smiled to himself before taking a fresh cube of ice from the bucket and with deliberately tantalising slowness drew it down the middle of her silk-covered sex-lips.

The ice-cold dampness against her over-heated flesh made Rowena groan. When the ice-cube was removed Chris scratched delicately against the material with his finger nails, and whenever he scratched over the clitoris Rowena's belly jerked and her legs trembled violently.

He continued to alternate the ice-cubes and his fingers and mouth on both her breasts and her vulva, and every time she came he would tighten the material between her legs until finally it was drawn up so hard against her that it slipped between her outer sex-lips and clung to the sticky inner lips, inexhorably stimulating the entire area.

Rowena began to scream at her half-brother, pleading with him to take her, to satisfy her properly, but he ignored her. Instead he dipped his tongue into her navel and swirled it around there, arousing yet more of her screaming nerve endings and causing another violent contraction of her internal muscles.

Harriet had lost count of the number of times the film star had been brought to orgasm by her own half-brother. She watched with rising excitement as the woman writhed, sobbed and threw her head around in what seemed to be a world of total pleasure, but a dark, forbidden pleasure that Harriet had never imagined existing. Next to her, Lewis put a hand on her knee and squeezed softly. 'Arousing, don't you think?'

'But they're related!' she exclaimed.

'They share the same father, yes.'

'Don't you mind?' she asked in astonishment.

'I find it very interesting,' was all he said.

Back in the bedroom, Chris decided the game had gone on long enough. Putting his hands round Rowena's waist he pulled her to her feet, pushed her head down and then withdrew the plughead from between her curved buttocks. He heard her sharp intake of breath as the bulbous head was finally removed and felt his own erection harden still more.

'Bend over the end of the bed,' he said hoarsely, and as she obeyed him he let his trousers drop to the floor, drew the damp, clinging material out of her sex-lips, pushed it to one side then thrust into her back passage himself.

As he drove into her, Rowena frantically caressed her own nipples by writhing on the bedspread while Chris used his fingers to stimulate her clitoris, at last giving it the firmer pressure that it had been screaming for throughout the game.

Rowena struggled to keep her final cresting orgasm at bay, knowing that in this game Chris always had to come first during the final session. To her horror he seemed to be lasting longer than ever before and she could feel her body swelling and the burning darts of pleasure streaked through her at an increasing rate until finally she reached the point of no return and with a despairing scream she toppled over the edge and let the climax tear through her.

Her resulting spasms were reflected in the walls of her rectum and as they tightened around Chris he lost his self-control and felt his seed rising upwards in a flood until with a shuddering gasp he was releasing himself into her still twitching body.

The moment he'd finished he withdrew, his face dark with anger. 'You came first!' he said accusingly.

Rowena struggled to turn over and looked up at him apologetically. 'I couldn't help it, Chris. You'd done everything too well, I just lost control.'

'Then I'll make you lose control again.'

'No, I've had enough. I can't,' she begged, but Chris was beyond stopping. Covering the fingers of his right hand in lubricating jelly he began to massage it into her exhausted tissue, spreading it around the sides and base of her clitoris until she was squirming once more.

'Let me see you come again,' he demanded.

Rowena closed her eyes and gave herself over to his touch, but her flesh was tired and she couldn't reach the peak he was asking of her. Infuriated, Chris knelt down and then she felt his tongue licking round the entrance to her vagina and the heat of an orgasm began to spread through her belly.

'Yes! Yes!' she whimpered.

His tongue snaked inside her, swirled around with the lightest of touches and slowly she felt herself melting into a pool of liquid. The heat increased, spread upwards through her entire body and her head went back hard into the mattress. 'I'm coming now!' she gasped.

Chris withdrew his tongue and stood up. 'I've changed my mind,' he said coldly. 'I think you were right, you'd had enough already.' With that he turned and left the room, leaving Rowena with her hands still tied behind her, lying on the bed screaming at him to come back and finish what he'd begun.

Harriet watched the internationally renowned screen goddess struggling fruitlessly to free her hands and turned to Lewis, sitting silently beside her. 'Will Chris come back?' she whispered.

'He won't need to. Rowena's very resourceful. I'm sure she'll manage on her own. She has the additional incentive of knowing that she can't afford to let her maid discover her like that in the morning.'

Harriet was shocked by his casual acceptance of what they'd seen. Rowena was his wife, and even an open marriage didn't usually include letting your wife have sex with her half-brother. She decided he was simply good at hiding his emotions, and that this was the only way he could cope with the situation.

She was wrong. Lewis was drawn to Rowena sexually; like most men he admired her body and found her sexual magnetism alluring, but emotionally he was untouched by her. Their marriage had suited him as much as it suited her. The joining together of his analytical, much-admired director's brain and her renowned sexuality and beauty had attracted almost as much attention in Hollywood as Marilyn Monroe's marriage to Arthur Miller.

Looking into the bedroom again, Harriet realised that Rowena's first priority didn't seem to be freedom from her bonds so much as freedom from her frustration, for once she failed to loosen her wrists she got to her feet and stood in front of one of the bed-posts. She pressed herself against it, thrusting her pelvis forward so that her silk-encased vulva rubbed against the rounded, patterned wood and as she found her rhythm her head went back and her red-gold hair streamed down the gentle curve of her back.

Neither Harriet nor Lewis could hear anything, but they could both imagine the sounds she would be making as the tension mounted in her rounded body until with a long shudder she finally reached the summit of pleasure and her muscles went rigid before gradually dissolving into relaxed softness once her body was calm again.

For a few minutes Rowena stayed leaning against the bed-post, her eyes half-closed and her breathing ragged, but then, still totally unaware of the onlookers, she set her mind to the problem of her bound wrists. Glancing round the room she saw the sharp edges of her drinks cabinet. The silk cords were slim and it only took a few minutes of rubbing against one of the edges before they broke and she was finally free.

She massaged each of the red marks lightly, taking perverse pleasure from the stinging pain as the blood-flow was restored. She was annoyed with Chris, but not as annoyed as she was with Lewis. That afternoon, when he'd been making love to Harriet, he'd done it with a tenderness and enthusiasm she hadn't expected and it had unsettled her.

Until now she'd taken Lewis for granted. She knew he wasn't in love with her but he liked being married to her and she liked having him as a husband. His love-making was excellent, and his detached, calm temperament was the perfect foil for all her insecurities.

If only she'd been able to give up Chris then none of this would be happening, she mused as she slipped into a satin nightdress and began to brush her hair. She had been certain that after a time Lewis would make Chris unnecessary to her, but it hadn't happened. Chris knew her body better than any other man, and Lewis either couldn't or wouldn't do the things that Chris did for her.

As Lewis became more successful and his work took him away from her for weeks at a time she'd turned increasingly to Chris, and had felt her marriage slipping away. When Lewis had suggested the film, explaining that through it the two of them would resolve their situation, she'd been as enthusiastic as him. Certainly watching him with Harriet had aroused unexpected feelings of jealousy, but tonight when Chris had almost forced himself on her she'd known that her need for Chris had been increased by what they'd witnessed earlier that day. It should have had the opposite effect, she should have wanted Lewis more and Chris less, but Chris was her comfort. He was always there, always able to stimulate and ultimately soothe her. There was another reason as well; Chris liked Harriet.

Rowena knew that Lewis had chosen Harriet because he'd been attracted to her – the plot could scarcely work if the second woman wasn't one that he fancied – but she hadn't for a moment considered the possibility that Chris would like her too.

Tonight, as her half-brother had tantalised and tormented her to higher and higher peaks of delight, she'd had the terrible feeling that at the back of his mind he was picturing Harriet in her place. She didn't know if it was just paranoia or her usually reliable sixth sense, but right now, at the very start of Lewis's story when the plot was only just starting to unfold, Rowena found herself horribly afraid.

Before she slid beneath the sheets she glanced at herself in the full-length mirror. She still looked stunning and sexy, she told herself, and it was true, in which case she shouldn't be worrying. Harriet was there to push Rowena into making a choice between the men, not as a threat to her relationship with them both. The sooner she remembered that and used her considerable assets the more certain she could feel that the outcome would suit her and not Harriet.

After all, she told herself as she drifted off to sleep, Harriet was nothing special. Young and attractive, yes, but hardly in the same league as an international sex symbol. The thought comforted her, although not as much as she'd hoped.

Lewis and Harriet remained in their seats until Rowena's head was on her pillow, her eyes closed in readiness for sleep, then Lewis rose to his feet. 'There, perhaps now you won't feel so guilty about our affair.'

'How long has it been going on?' asked a stunned Harriet.

'The affair with Chris? Ever since they were teenagers. Their father was married to Chris's mother when he got Rowena's mother pregnant. There are only twelve months between them. When Chris was three their father left his family and went to live with Rowena and her mother. When Chris was ten his mother died and he joined his father's second family. Obviously the two children became close. I don't think either of the adults had much time for the pair of them and they relied on each other for everything. Once their bodies started to mature the inevitable happened.'

'But once they were old enough to know it was wrong, why didn't they stop?' asked Harriet.

Lewis smiled to himself in the darkness. 'We all have special needs, Harriet. Dark, hidden desires that we don't feel we can reveal to the world. Chris and Rowena have no fear of each other; their relationship is totally open. Family genes seem to have meant that their needs are remarkably similar, they complement each other perfectly. Why should they have stopped?'

By this time he and Harriet were standing on the landing and he put both his hands on her shoulders, feeling her quivering beneath his touch. She'd been aroused by what they'd seen, just as he had, but for tonight she would have to wait. Their love-making, when it happened, would be all the sweeter for the delay.

'Because it's wrong!' exclaimed Harriet.

'That isn't a view that I subscribe to,' said Lewis. 'The only thing I insist on is that I take precedence. In sexual matters a husband should come before a half-brother, don't you agree?'

Harriet moved away from him, suddenly wanting nothing more to do with this dark, sexually magnetic man who seemed totally untroubled by moral scruples. 'You must be very broad-minded indeed to be able to make jokes about it,' she said shortly. 'Either that or you don't care about Rowena.'

'Perhaps I don't.'

Harriet hesitated at the top of the stairs. 'Did you ever?' she asked curiously.

'I really can't remember,' said Lewis.

*

Dark Secret

The next morning as Rowena dictated numerous letters to Harriet, Lewis was closeted in his study with Mark, his scriptwriter for *Dark Secret*.

'Okay,' said Mark, lighting up one of his cigars. 'So we've had the sex scene between the husband and the secretary. What happens next?'

'Next I think the wife and her brother will make passionate love.'

Mark shook his head. 'No, it doesn't ring true. If the wife and the brother had been watching the husband and the secretary then the wife would be jealous. She'd start trying to think of ways to get the husband into her bed, not roll around with her brother.'

'I think you're wrong.'

'Why?' asked Mark.

Lewis thought for a moment. 'Perhaps because she's always turned to her brother when she's been troubled. Or looking at it from another point of view, perhaps the brother's turned on by what he's been watching and he forces himself on his only slightly reluctant sister. Yes, that's the way it should go.'

'You mean the brother fancies the secretary too?'

'Not necessarily, he might just have been aroused by the sex itself.'

'So the brother doesn't fancy the second woman?'

Lewis grinned. 'He might in time, I'm not sure yet.'

Mark sighed. 'It's bloody difficult writing it this way. If I had more of an idea of how the whole thing was going to develop I could slant the dialogue that way. You know, give subtle pointers to the audience.'

'I don't want the plot to be signposted. I want it to unfold slowly, giving its secrets a little at a time; rather like a Woman when you think about it.'

'You're the boss,' muttered Mark, clearly unhappy with the way things were going. 'So, what kind of a sex scene is this one?'

Lewis pretended to think about the question for a moment or two. 'Mild bondage, pseudo-force, that kind of thing.'

'Who gets tied up?'

'The woman,' said Lewis with a sigh. 'Didn't I say at the beginning that this was the way her brother kept her tied to him.'

Mark laughed. 'You meant literally!'

Lewis's face went cold. 'If you don't want the job, Mark, there are plenty of other equally good scriptwriters I could use.'

Mark quickly stopped laughing. 'Hey, Lewis, it was

a joke. You know I want the job. It's weird, but it's sure as hell different.'

'Good. Bring it over to me when you've finished the scene. By then I should know what direction I want it to take after that.'

'And Rowena's really going to star in this?' asked Mark.

'She can't wait,' Lewis assured him. 'Don't forget the dinner party on Saturday, will you.'

In the front room Rowena heard the door slam and saw Mark walking towards his car. She bit on her lower lip, wondering what Lewis had said to him and how different the plot would have been if he'd seen her and Chris last night.

She felt guilty about that. Not about what they'd done together but about the fact that she hadn't told Lewis. How could his film be truthful if he didn't know everything? For a moment she thought about admitting it all, but changed her mind again. It wasn't as though she'd wanted it to happen, it had been at Chris's instigation and she'd just given in. Lewis was only interested in Rowena's reactions.

'Anything else?' asked Harriet politely.

Rowena looked blankly at her.

'You were in the middle of a letter. You'd just said ...'

'Leave that one. You've plenty of others to type,' said Rowena, suddenly anxious to see her husband. 'I'll sign them after lunch.'

Harriet stood up, closing her notebook and giving her employer a quick smile. Rowena noticed that Harriet's skirt was far shorter than the ones she'd been wearing, and that her silk top clung to her breasts in a distinctly provocative way.

'You look different today,' she said abruptly.

Harriet, who felt different, tried not to blush. 'I thought this outfit would be more comfortable. It's much warmer today.'

'That explains why you've left your tights off,' murmured Rowena. 'If you want to top up your tan you can always use the sunbed. It's in a cubicle off the swimming pool.' Harriet thanked her and went away to start typing.

Rowena checked her appearance in the mirror above the fireplace, then went along to Lewis's study. He was sitting at his desk writing in longhand, and when she came into the room he pushed the papers into a folder. 'I thought you were busy this morning, darling.'

112

Rowena perched on the edge of his desk and bent slightly forward, giving him an excellent view of her perfect cleavage. 'I've finished dictating now. I thought perhaps we could talk about the film.'

'There's nothing to talk about. You saw what happened yesterday afternoon. That's the only scene I've got so far.'

'Did you enjoy making love to her?' asked Rowena.

Lewis stared into her bright blue eyes. 'Yes, very much. She was gratifyingly responsive.'

'More responsive than I am?'

'I didn't say that.'

'Make love to me now,' said Rowena, sliding off the desk and moving round so that she could sit on his lap.

'I have to spend my time with Harriet,' Lewis reminded her. 'If the next part of our plan is to succeed then it's vital that for the next few days I concentrate on pleasuring her. Her body must get used to me. When I stop visiting her, her body has to be left screaming for satisfaction. It's the only way we'll get her to go along with us.'

Rowena had heard all this many months earlier, but it hadn't mattered then because at that time the second woman hadn't been chosen. It was different now that Harriet was in the house.

'You've never been a once-a-day man,' she whispered to Lewis, pulling his swivel chair round so that he was facing her and sitting on his thighs, her legs hanging down on either side of him. 'Surely you've still got some energy left for me?'

Lewis eyed her curiously. Her black and red Lycra dress clung to every curve and the self-tie halter top was too tempting to be ignored. It was plain to him that she'd intended to have him from the moment she got up that morning, otherwise she would have been wearing her normal work-type clothes of designer jeans and cropped top.

Slowly his arms went round her and his hands slid up her back so that he could unfasten the dress. His fingers were quick and deft and within seconds he was peeling the top forward, revealing her rounded breasts, their nipples already partly erect.

Rowena gave a sigh of satisfaction and pulled his head down. She wanted to feel his long tongue against her, needed the gentle grazing of his teeth against her straining nipples. Lewis let her have her way. He moved his head from side to side so that his tongue could harden each of the rosy peaks in turn and then he drew her right nipple carefully into his mouth and sucked lightly until he felt her squirming against his thighs.

Her dress rode up her legs and he realised that she hadn't bothered to put on any underwear except stockings. His excitement increased and he felt himself hardening. Suddenly he wanted to take her quickly and violently right now, without any further preliminaries, and his right hand went to his zip to free his imprisoned erection.

Rowena made a soft sound of pleasure and lifted her hips to accommodate him, at the same time pressing her breasts more firmly against his face. Lewis slid into her and his hands grasped her by the hips in order to move her at the pace he wanted.

Rowena's eyes closed and she reached a hand down between their bodies to stimulate her clitoris as Lewis continued to move her up and down in an increasingly rapid rhythm.

At the touch of her own fingers on the slowly swelling bud, Rowena began to shiver and tiny tendrils of excitement started to snake their way up through her stomach. Lewis nibbled gently on the nipple in his

mouth and this extra sensation gave Rowena the stimulation her climax seemed to need.

She felt it throbbing between her thighs like a pulse
beating beneath the paper-thin skin of her perineum,
and knew that she was about to come. Lewis was
aware of it too and he let the fingers of his hands dig
firmly into her hips.

'Yes, yes!' she shouted and her body began to arch
away from him so that he had to tighten his grip on her
hips in order to keep her in position.

At that moment there was a light tap on the study
door and Harriet walked in. 'Lewis, have you seen
Rowena? I can't find her anywhere and she's wanted on
the telephone.'

Chapter Five

LEWIS STARED AT Harriet, hiding his anger behind a mask of indifference. Inwardly he was raging, not only at the fact that she had come into the room uninvited but also at his own stupidity in allowing Rowena to persuade him to make love to her at a time when he should have been concentrating solely on Harriet.

'Rowena will be with you in a moment,' he said smoothly, his arousal dissipating at great speed.

Harriet's eyes were wide and she stared at her employer as Rowena, ignoring the younger woman's presence, continued to move herself up and down on Lewis until with a cry of pleasure her body gave itself over to the warm flooding joy of orgasm.

Harriet knew that she should leave the room but her legs seemed unable to move. She stayed rooted to the spot watching Rowena's total abandonment to her sexuality. She felt almost consumed by envy, having spent most of her waking hours imagining what her next sexual encounter with Lewis would be like. Now she was forced to face the fact that he was pleasuring his wife at the same time, despite what he had seen her doing the previous night.

For a moment she wavered, thought of leaving the house and turning her back on all of them. Their way of life and lack of what she considered morality were so alien to her she didn't now how she could stay. But then she looked at Lewis, still watching her over his wife's head and she knew that she couldn't go. She wanted this man more than she'd ever wanted anyone and if possible she intended to take him away from Rowena.

This revelation was a shock to Harriet. She knew that it was illogical, that so far he'd only made love to her once and that he probably anticipated losing interest in her once the novelty had worn off, but watching him with Rowena, seeing those golden hands caressing her body, she decided that regardless of how impossible it seemed she would have her way. She would be very careful how she went about it though, since Lewis must think he was the hunter.

Lewis saw Harriet's eyes changing, and wondered what was going through her head. He hoped she wasn't planning to leave them, not just when everything was going so well. Cursing the fact that Rowena had wound her arms round his neck and was nestling against his chest like a small child, probably in order to remind Harriet that this was her husband, he raised his eyebrows apologetically at the silent girl.

'I'll ask the caller to ring back,' said Harriet, delighted to find that her voice sounded rock steady.

'That would be helpful,' said Lewis politely. He wondered if Harriet felt as ridiculous as he did carrying out such a banal conversation considering the scene she'd just witnessed.

'I'm sorry I interrupted,' Harriet added. 'I thought you called for me to come in. Obviously I was wrong.'

'Has she gone?' demanded Rowena when she heard the door close.

Lewis sighed. 'Yes, I only hope she doesn't decide to go for good.'

Rowena laughed and sat back on his lap, her eyes bright and her cheeks flushed. 'Surely you didn't tell her we never slept together? Even Harriet wouldn't fall for an old cliche like that!'

'Of course I didn't, but this shouldn't have happened.'

Rowena stretched voluptuously and kissed him on the side of his neck. 'I'm very glad it did; it was delicious. I wonder who this call was from?'

Lewis, frustrated both sexually and by the turn of events, couldn't have cared less. 'You'd better go and find out,' he said shortly. 'And for God's sake don't go talking about this to Harriet. Keep a dignified silence. The pair of you aren't meant to talk about anything intimate at this stage in the plot.'

'Don't worry, I've got the outline safely in my head.'

'If you let me down over this, Rowena, I'll never forgive you,' said Lewis seriously. 'It has to be done properly, otherwise it will be just another film. I want it to be a true story.'

'I was just having a little rehearsal for one of the scenes,' laughed his wife, sliding from his lap. 'Will you be at lunch or are you planning another afternoon session with my PA?'

'After this I'll be lucky to get into her room tonight,' he said gloomily.

When Rowena returned to Harriet's office she found her typing efficiently, but when she lifted her head to speak to Rowena the grey eyes held a look that troubled the film star. It wasn't anger, which she'd half-expected, and nor was it envy; it was almost a sympathetic look.

'Who rang?' demanded Rowena abruptly.

'They didn't say, but it was an American man.'

'An American? Perhaps it was my agent. Why didn't you …?'

'I tried to tell you it was important, but you were very busy,' said Harriet calmly.

It was Rowena's turn to change colour and she had to go to her room and sit quietly trying to visualise a peaceful summer scene, as her personal physician had suggested, before she could calm herself. If it had been her agent he might have work for her, work that would be less emotionally demanding than this venture of Lewis's. But then again, it wasn't likely to carry the chance of an Oscar, and an Oscar was something Rowena yearned for.

Lewis stayed in his study for the rest of the day, only leaving it once to go for a walk in the grounds. Harriet saw him from her office window, strolling across the grass with his hands in his pockets and his head bent in thought.

Even the way he moved aroused her. His long, smooth stride and the tightness of his buttocks beneath his trousers reminded her of the way he looked naked. His bronze-coloured body, his dark hair and eyes made her stomach flutter with excitement. She wondered why it was that he had this effect on her.

Dinner that night consisted of roast chicken cooked with lemon and tarragon followed by a passion fruit sorbet. This time Rowena ate hungrily and it was Harriet who picked at her food, her appetite dulled by her sexual hunger for Lewis.

Chris watched Harriet with interest. He knew as well as Rowena did the way the plot was meant to unravel and could hardly wait for the moment when he was able to take her himself. She would be so different from Rowena, hopefully reluctant to accept the ways he used to pleasure his women. The prospect of her reluctance and the knowledge that in the end she would almost certainly submit caused him to harden, and he decided that if Lewis was going to have her again that night then he would watch. This time he wouldn't take Rowena with him either.

'You're quiet, Chris,' said Rowena suddenly.

'I went down to the gym this afternoon and worked out for a couple of hours; I'm exhausted,' he said with a grin.

Lewis glanced at him. 'Which gym?'

'Luigi's.'

'That's funny; when I spoke to him on the phone earlier he didn't mention seeing you, and it would have been something of an event, don't you agree?'

'Well I was there,' lied Chris, who'd really been round all the sex shops he could find, buying additional equipment for his collection.

'More wine, Harriet?' asked Lewis.

She nodded. It dulled the fear that he wasn't going to make love to her again unless she made a move, and at the moment she didn't know what kind of a move to make. As he filled her glass his head moved close to hers. I'll come to your room at eleven,' he whispered.

Harriet didn't take in much of the conversation that followed his promise. Her hand trembled when she raised the wine glass to her lips and she found it hard to stop herself watching Lewis all the time. Across the table from her, Chris continued to study Harriet. He'd seen Lewis murmur something and noted the effect of his words. Despite her cool, controlled exterior he already knew that she was a deeply sexual person; now it seemed that her emotions were involved as well. He was starting to enjoy Lewis's plot more with every moment that passed.

Dinner ended at nine-thirty. While the other three took coffee in the drawing-room, Harriet excused herself and went up to her bedroom. There she had a long bath, using the expensive bath oil and body lotion that had been left for her. Then she washed her hair with a jasmine-scented shampoo and conditioner before blow-drying it, using her fingers as a comb so that instead of falling in a sleek curtain to her shoulders it looked tousled and casual.

Finally she dabbed some Worth perfume, a present from James the previous Christmas, behind her ears, beneath her breasts and at the back of her knees before pulling on an ankle-length jade silk peignoir over a matching nightdress.

By the time she'd finished another hour had passed but she still had thirty minutes to kill. She spent them working out ways in which she could give Lewis pleasure as well as letting him give it to her.

When he finally tapped on the door she was in a

state of intense anticipation. The bath, the massaging of her own body with the lotion and the feel of the silk against her warm flesh had all heightened her senses. She longed for him with a hunger so intense it actually hurt her physically.

Lewis eyed her appreciatively and then kissed her on the temples. 'You smell delicious,' he murmured. 'Good enough to eat, I think.'

As he slipped the peignoir off her shoulders, Harriet started to unfasten the buttons of his shirt and he stood compliantly, letting her undress him while his hands continually touched and stroked her body.

When he was finally naked she put her hands on his chest and pushed him towards the bed. He looked slightly surprised but obeyed, then stretched out on his back. 'I take it you've got something special in mind?' he said with a smile.

'I want to make you as happy as you make me,' she whispered.

Lewis was intrigued by this turn of events. It hadn't entered his mind that she would start to take the initiative so early, but the very fact that she had excited him, and he felt his penis swelling rapidly until it was fully erect.

Harriet slid the shoulder straps of her nightdress off and let them fall teasingly down her arms. From the bed Lewis watched, his eyes growing dark with desire. Then she wriggled her hips and the garment fell to the floor leaving her as naked as he was.

Now she joined him on the bed and lay on top of him with her head on his stomach. Since his penis was straining upwards this put her in the perfect position to take it in her mouth and she heard his swift intake of breath as her tongue swept round the circumference of his glans while her lips applied gentle suction.

The surprise of what she was doing, coupled with the sensations her mouth was causing him, made self-control difficult for Lewis. He knew that if their love-making was to last he must distract himself slightly, without stopping Harriet doing what she wanted to do.

His hands caressed the rounded cheeks of her bottom, so tantalisingly displayed for him, and moved up over her hips then round to her belly. Her skin rippled beneath his touch and when he let his fingers brush fleetingly against her vulva he could feel that her outer lips had opened up and she was damp with desire.

He moistened a finger in her liquid excitement and as she began to move her head up and down along the shaft of his penis he very slowly inserted the tip of the finger into the tiny puckered opening between the pale globes in front of him.

For a moment Harriet froze. No one had ever touched her there, and she wasn't certain that she wanted Lewis to, but then the gentle pressure sent a new and different kind of pleasure through her and as her body tightened all the nerve endings around her clitoris were indirectly stimulated so that the excitement was doubled.

After her slight hesitation Lewis felt Harriet relax again, and he continued this form of stimulation for her while his penis began to strain under the continuous pleasuring, until he knew that if he left it a moment longer he would lose control. Putting his hands on her waist he pulled softly. 'That's enough, Harriet. I don't want the evening to end yet, you know.'

She felt a thrill of excitement at this proof of her power over him and reluctantly slid her mouth along the saliva-dampened shaft one final time as she released him. He felt her tongue dip into the tiny slit at the tip as she lapped at the droplet of pre-ejaculatory fluid gathered there, and that small touch nearly finished him.

The well trained muscles of his abdomen fought to subdue his increasing need to climax and he pulled Harriet off him before she could torment him further with her mouth.

'Now it's my turn,' he whispered in her ear, and her body seemed to swell at the words. Turning her on to her belly he pushed two pillows beneath it. This meant that her buttocks were thrust high into the air and he then pulled her legs wider apart until she was totally open to him. Harriet wriggled with delicious excitement.

'Keep still,' he said, his voice thick with sexual hunger. 'Only move when I say you can.'

The very command added to her need to move. Lying still seemed an impossibility and yet she did as he said because she knew that it would add an extra dimension to her final satisfaction.

Taking a slim vibrator from the bedside drawer, Lewis put it on the lowest setting and then very softly let it massage Harriet's perineum. As she felt the soft tingling sensation in the skin between her front and back passages Harriet thrust her buttocks still higher, only to feel a slight burning sensation as Lewis flicked her with his fingers. 'I said keep still,' he reminded her.

Startled by the stinging flick she immediately lay motionless, and it was then that Lewis increased the vibrator's speed and let it roam around her clitoris, avoiding the hard little knot of nerve endings itself but concentrating on the sensitive tissue surrounding it.

Harriet longed to move, her hips secmed to have taken on a life of their own, and as the nerve endings sent thrilling messages of pleasure to her brain she had to fight to still her movements. It was agony, but exquisite agony, and lack of movement meant that she was even more aware of the incredible sensations that were engulfing her.

Lewis watched her carefully, admiring the way she kept her hips still and her acceptance of this new sexual game, so clearly not a part of her previous experience.

Her breathing was audible and ragged as the pressure within her increased and her tight stomach was further stimulated by the pillows beneath it, pillows that positively invited her to press deep into them and

gain further satisfaction, an invitation she knew Lewis
would not expect her to accept.

When she was fully in control of herself, enjoying the
glorious streaks of ecstasy and the mounting heaviness
deep within her core, Lewis decided to add more stimulation. Slowly he slid the head of the vibrator down
her damp, slippery channel and into the hungry opening of her vagina. At the same time he lowered his head
and let his tongue take over from the vibrator around
her clitoris.

Harriet felt like screaming at the new sensation.
Lewis started to vary the speeds of the vibrator. When
he slowed it down he slowed the movement of his
tongue, quickening them both in unison as soon as her
body had adjusted to the more rapid touch. As the
stimulation continued she lost all sense of what was
happening to her, all she could concentrate on were the
mounting waves of excitement and the increasingly
rapid pulse beating behind the clitoris itself.

Her stomach ached it was so tight and tense, and she
heard herself pleading with Lewis to allow her to move
but he flicked his fingers against her inner thighs and
she knew the burning stinging sensation was his
answer. Suddenly all the sparks of sensation, all the

sharp darts and tendrils of arousal, began to join together and Lewis saw the cheeks of her bottom tighten as her orgasm approached.

'Keep still a moment longer,' he whispered to the straining Harriet, and then he withdrew the vibrator and with one abrupt thrusting movement allowed his rampant erection to slide into her, taking care to keep up the stimulation of her clitoris with his fingers instead of his tongue.

Harriet felt that she was going to explode. Her body was being racked by liquid fire and then the incessant drumming of the pulse between her legs changed to a startlingly intense tingling that felt hot and rushed upwards through her with terrifying speed.

She shouted out loud, knowing that she could no longer keep her body still even to please this man who meant so much to her.

At the sound Lewis moved his fingers to the side of her clitoris and rubbed the slippery tissue with tiny circular motions as he moved in and out of her, his own body straining for relief from the continuous sexual tension as much as Harriet's.

It was Harriet who came first and as her body went taut with the first fierce contractions of her orgasm her vaginal walls contracted tightly around Lewis so that she felt as though she was milking him. She heard him groan and then he was thrusting without thought for her, thrusting solely to give himself the satisfaction that he knew Harriet was about to get.

Harriet's climax, having been delayed so long, built to a crescendo and then stopped, keeping her body tight and balanced on the edge of release for so long that she wondered how it was possible to bear such pleasure. Then it flooded through her and she felt the resulting explosion in every part of her, even her fingers and toes tingling with the final orgasmic convulsion.

Beads of sweat covered Lewis's forehead and upper lip and for a moment he looked down at Harriet's supine body with an expression of surprise on his face. Even for him it had been an unusually intense orgasm and he wondered why it had been so good.

Harriet, unable to see his face since her head was still buried in the duvet, longed for him to say something loving, something to show that it had been special for him, but all he did was lie down next to her and draw her to him, soothing and petting her with his large hands.

Through the peephole, Chris continued his silent vigil. His own excitement was so great that he could scarcely control it, but he had no intention of going to Rowena tonight. He wanted to lie in his bed and think about Harriet. She'd been wonderful with Lewis, obeying his every command and showing depths of passion that were amazing, but it wasn't the same as it would be when Chris finally got to have her.

Then the instructions would be orders, and disobedience would be punished by more than a gentle flick of the fingers. He wondered how she would respond to that kind of sexual game. As for Lewis, his behaviour had been intriguing. Chris had seen his brother-in-law making love to Rowena in all kinds of ways but he'd never seen him so involved. The man had always appeared detached, taking his sexual pleasure in much the same way as through food or drink. Tonight he had let himself lose control, and the final soothing of the post-orgasmic Harriet showed far more concern for her as a person than Chris would have expected. All in all he thought it was a very interesting situation.

Half an hour later Lewis left Harriet asleep in her bed and went downstairs to his study. From there he telephoned Mark, who answered the phone sounding sleepy and irritable.

'I want you over here now,' said Lewis.

'Bloody hell, Lew, do you know what time it is?'

'Since you scarcely work in the day at the moment I don't think that matters. Get here and make it fast.'

'What's the urgency?' demanded Mark twenty minutes later after Lewis had let him in to the silent house.

'I've had this idea and I want to sound it out on you.'

'You're the boss.'

'That's right,' said Lewis with a smile that didn't reach his eyes. 'I am. Now, let's say that after making love to her brother our heroine decides that she wants to seduce her husband.'

'She doesn't have to seduce him, they're married,' objected Mark.

'Yes, but this *is* a seduction. She could go to his office and make love to him there, something like that.'

'On the desk top you mean? That always looks a bit tacky.'

'Okay,' agreed Lewis, smiling to himself. 'Not the desk then, let's say she just lifts her dress and sits on his lap while he's sitting in his chair.'

'Sounds good to me.'

'Fine, then at the vital moment, when they're both

approaching the point of no return, the secretary walks in.'

'Why?' asked Mark. 'Surely she'd knock first?'

'Right, so we'll make her knock but she takes the sounds of passion coming from inside as permission to enter.'

Mark grinned. 'I like it! Then what?'

'This is a bit difficult, but I think she'll stay and watch.'

'Miss Super Secretary doesn't turn tail and run?' exclaimed Mark.

'No, she might like to, in fact we'd better make her show she'd like to, but the eroticism of the scene stops her from moving.'

'And how does the wife react?' queried Mark.

Lewis smiled. 'I think the wife would feel rather pleased with herself. After all, this girl is a threat and she knows it. How better to reduce the threat than to show the intruder that her husband can still be so overwhelmed with lust for his wife that he can't wait for the privacy of their bedroom?'

'But won't the next meeting between the two women be awkward?'

'Of course it will. The wife naturally expects the

secretary to be miserable, but I don't want that to happen. I want the secretary to unsettle the wife.'

'How?'

Lewis sighed. 'That's the trouble, I'm not sure. By accepting it all, I suppose. She can carry on as though nothing's happened – that would make the wife feel uncomfortable. If someone doesn't behave in the way you've anticipated it's always unsettling.'

'You think Miss Super Secretary is capable of handling it like that this early on?'

Lewis nodded. 'Yes, I do. In fact, to underline that nothing's changed, she and the husband can have another passionate encounter that very night.'

Mark grinned. 'So the husband's a bit of a superman!'

'No, he's just highly sexed. Besides, isn't it every man's fantasy to have two women in his house, both of them anxious for his sexual favours?'

'It wouldn't be mine,' said Mark, scribbling down notes. 'In my experience women have a habit of coming off best in any situation, even one like this.'

'That's not the ending I've got in mind,' said Lewis shortly.

'You mean you know how it's going to end? I thought you were working this out a step at a time.'

'I am.' Lewis's voice was irritable now. 'That doesn't mean I don't have a final objective in view, but you're right, the plot might not develop the way I think.'

Mark stared at the director for a moment, wondering exactly what was going on in this house, but it wasn't his place to ask questions and already he had the gut feeling that the film was going to be something really special. 'What time's dinner on Saturday?' he asked as he put his notes away.

'Eight-thirty for nine. Don't bring anyone; we've got a spare woman coming.'

'I hope she's good-looking.'

'She's probably hoping the same about you!' laughed Lewis, and as he showed Mark out he made a mental note to himself to invite Harriet to join them. He wanted Mark to see her, if only to discover whether or not Mark guessed how Lewis was working on his plot. Closing the front door quietly, Lewis finally went up to his room to sleep.

In the morning Rowena was in a foul mood. She didn't appear until the others had finished breakfast, then when she finally joined them there were dark shadows beneath her eyes and her face looked puffy.

'Bad night?' asked Lewis after one quick glance.

'Yes, I couldn't sleep. Even the pills didn't work.'

'You'd better have a facial.'

Rowena glared at her husband. 'I know I look bad, you don't have to rub it in.'

'I didn't say that. Facials always relax you. Do you need me for anything this morning, only I'd planned to go out for a couple of hours. People to see, papers to sign, that kind of thing. And this afternoon I'll need to borrow Harriet.'

'I'm sure Harriet won't mind, will you?' responded Rowena.

Harriet smiled at Lewis. 'I'd be delighted.'

The smile irritated Rowena even more. 'Unless you intend to work your way through another pot of coffee perhaps you could go through some of those letters from agents representing authors who want to do my authorised biography,' she said curtly. 'Weed out anyone who hasn't already done at least two, and check the names against my hate list.'

'Hate list?' Harriet was bewildered.

'My beloved sister keeps a list of all the people she's offended along her climb to stardom. She's terrified one of them will come back and wreak vengeance one day,' explained Chris.

'Do you think you can manage that?' demanded Rowena.

Harriet nodded, turned to leave and bumped into Lewis, who had turned to go at the same time. His hands caught her arm and for a moment his grip tightened into intimacy, which set her blood racing. 'Sorry!' he apologised, and then with a wink he was gone.

Rowena missed the byplay, but her half-brother didn't. Once the pair of them were alone he considered mentioning it, then decided there was no point. He hated it when Rowena got in a bad mood and always tried to bring her out of it.

'What are you staring at?' Rowena demanded.

Chris smiled his lazy smile. 'I was admiring your outfit.'

Rowena was wearing a short, figure-hugging black skirt, a lace trimmed black bra and a pure white linen overshirt that reached to her hips and was unbuttoned far enough to show the black bra peeping through. Once it would have been an unthinkable way of dressing, but Rowena was careful to keep up with new fashions and this look was very popular at the moment. It was also, as she appreciated very well, sexy.

'Where were you last night?' she muttered. 'I needed you.'

'I was asleep.'

'Liar! I rang your room and you didn't answer.'

'I don't answer the phone in my sleep.'

'Didn't you guess I was expecting you? I don't like what's happening; I don't know how to react or even what I really want. I've got to be able to depend on you still. We're always there for each other, you promised that wouldn't change.'

Chris tipped his chair back. 'I thought you wanted it to change. The whole idea of this film is to get you away from me, isn't it?'

'Just less dependent.' Rowena's voice was soft now, almost caressing as she started to play him like a fish. Her body lusted for him, for his urgent, harsh love-making, but she knew that he liked to hear how much he was wanted.

'It wouldn't appear to be working.'

'I know one thing,' said Rowena with total honesty. 'I hate having Harriet in the house. It's ridiculous, she was meant to be jealous of me and I'm becoming jealous of her.'

'It's a competition – of course you're jealous, but

you hold all the cards. Harriet's only a secondary player.'

'I hope she knows that,' said Rowena fiercely. She looked at Chris lounging back in his chair, his blond curls unbrushed and his light blue eyes continually flicking to her cleavage. 'Let's do it now, Chris,' she whispered.

'In here?'

'Why not? Harriet's busy, Lewis has gone out and I don't think I can wait until tonight. Please, Chris.'

He could never resist her. Their dependency was mutual and yet as he worked out how best to satisfy her in the confines of the breakfast room he found that he was imagining doing it with Harriet watching them. This idea added to his excitement and he felt himself growing hard.

'Crouch on the kitchen chair,' he said shortly. 'Put your feet on the seat and grip the back with your hands. If you thrust backwards I'll be able to stand on the floor and take you from behind.'

Rowena's mouth went dry. This was what she craved from him; swift, urgent couplings spiced with the risk of discovery were almost as satisfying to her as their long dark sessions where she allowed him to dominate her totally.

As she squatted on the chair, her feet as far apart as the seat would allow, her skirt rose up and Chris realised with a thrill of excitement that she was wearing crotchless panties. He put his hands on her waist and without any preliminaries at all thrust roughly into her.

As he thrust he put his mouth close to her ear and each time she was pushed forward by the force of him Rowena heard him whispering, 'You're mine, mine, do you hear?'

The words increased her excitement and she slid her right hand beneath the hem of her skirt so that she could stimulate herself but it was hardly necessary. Already her excitement was mounting and when Chris moved his hands upwards and cupped her breasts through the linen shirt she contracted the muscles of her pelvic floor with the result that her pre-orgasmic tremors intensified. As her half-brother muttered, 'I'll never let you go, never,' her body exploded in a dizzying mass of pleasure until she slumped forward with her head resting against the rounded top of the kitchen chair.

Chris leant against her back, his breathing gradually calming. When his erection had subsided he slid out of her and with one final tweak of her nipples stepped away, adjusting his clothing.

When he left her, when her body was physically separated from his, Rowena felt a shiver of fear. Suddenly she wanted him back inside her, not for the sex – she was sated now-but to reassure herself that they were still close.

Chris saw her tremble. 'What's the matter?'

'I don't know. I'm so afraid all the time.'

'It isn't your heart that's going to be broken, it's Harriet's. She's falling in love with Lewis.'

Rowena climbed down off the chair and pulled her skirt back into place. 'Don't be stupid, she doesn't know him except physically. Anyway, Harriet doesn't look to me like the kind of girl who falls in love. She's much too sensible – an admirable English virtue.'

'I think you're wrong, but it needn't worry you.'

'It would worry me if it were true,' responded Rowena, running a hand through Chris's hair in a proprietory manner. 'Men are susceptible to women who fall in love with them. It flatters their ego.'

'Lewis doesn't have an ego problem.'

Rowena smiled. 'All men have an ego problem. I'd

better go and see how Harriet's getting on. I was a bit short with her earlier.'

'She won't have minded. She expects you to be temperamental; it goes with the territory, as they say.'

Chris was right. Rowena's bad mood hadn't perturbed Harriet, particularly after Lewis had managed to touch her, however briefly. She wasn't foolish enough to imagine that he was in love with her, but she did think that he liked her as a person as well as a sexual partner.

His emotional detachment from Rowena was starting to show itself to her. Given his continuing lack of jealousy over his wife's extraordinary relationship with her half-brother this was beginning to seem the most logical explanation, and if his emotions weren't engaged anywhere else then so much the better for her.

At the same time as Harriet was working out a strategy to get the man she wanted, Lewis was finalising his plan for drawing Harriet deeper into the web they were all spinning around her. Her sexual response to him was gratifying, and with a body so clearly made for sex it should be easy to train it to expect constant satisfaction. Once that was done, once she was used to a full and satisfying sex-life, then he would leave her for a time.

It would be harder than he'd imagined because he enjoyed giving her pleasure but his enjoyment was of secondary importance to the film, and the film's plot meant that Harriet had to be persuaded to go a step further into the world inhabited by all who lived in the house in Regent's Park.

Probably the only member of the household without any worries at this time was Chris. He was thoroughly enjoying himself. Rowena was turning to him more, not less as he'd feared, while Harriet fascinated him as no woman apart from his half-sister had ever done. He knew that in time he'd be allowed to use her, because the film called for Rowena to watch and assist him in this.

Anticipation of that moment, coupled with Rowena's urgent need, meant that for the first time in his life he was totally content. He was also amused because he had the feeling that Lewis's plan, so cleverly contrived to remove Chris and drive Rowena into her husband's arms, was going to misfire, and what he wanted more than anything else in the world was to see Lewis fail at something.

Chapter Six

THAT EVENING CHRIS and Rowena went to the opera. Lewis hated opera. 'Good music spoilt by bad acting,' was his opinion and nothing he saw ever made him change his mind. After they'd gone he went in search of Harriet and found her reading a book in the comfort of the drawing-room.

'We've got the house to ourselves,' he said with a smile. 'How would you like a nice bath? We can use the tub in Rowena's bathroom – it's meant for two.'

Harriet lifted her eyes from the page. 'I had a shower this morning, thanks.'

For a moment Lewis couldn't believe he'd heard her correctly. 'You don't have to be dirty,' he said with a laugh. 'It's meant to be a sensual pleasure.'

Harriet smiled in an absent-minded way. 'I'm sure it would be, but I'm a bit tired tonight.'

Since nothing in his imaginary script had prepared Lewis for this he was totally at a loss. 'I'd like it,' he said slowly. 'Doesn't that matter to you?'

With a soft sigh Harriet put the book to one side. 'Of course it does, Lewis, but I'm sure I'm not the only woman in London who'd be willing to give you a bath.'

'You're the only one I want to give me a bath,' he replied, frantically trying to work out how to handle this.

'Then you'll have to settle for a shower,' she said gently.

Lewis stared at her. 'What's all this about, Harriet? I thought you were enjoying our affair as much as I am.'

'I am, but I'm not in the mood tonight.'

He cursed silently. The whole plot hinged on the fact that she found him irresistible, that her need for him was total and when he left her she had to be devastated. This cool woman sitting looking at him with a half-smile on her face seemed to have suddenly stepped out character.

Much to Lewis's amazement it dawned on him that he wasn't only put out because of this divergence from the plot. He was also disappointed for himself. Their times together had been good, and his enjoyment had probably equalled hers. To be rejected wasn't something that happened to him very often and neither was it usual for any rejection to matter.

Harriet watched the way Lewis hovered in the doorway. He seemed unable to accept her words and leave, but at the same time she sensed that it was almost beyond him to press any harder. His personal pride would be offended at the thought that he'd had to beg for sex from any woman.

After careful thought Lewis went and sat on the arm of Harriet's chair, then he tenderly stroked her hair and the side of her face. 'You're not ill, are you?'

She laughed. 'Do I have to be ill before I say no?'

'Of course not. I had the apparently incorrect idea that what we had was special for both of us. It's difficult for me to have my hopes for a wonderful evening dashed, that's all.'

It was hard for Harriet to maintain her attitude of indifference when he was touching her so tenderly, his hand massaging her scalp in slow easy movements before travelling in a lingering caress down her neck. Despite herself she began to tremble.

Lewis felt her reaction. 'Please, Harriet,' he said huskily. 'I don't know what your real reason is for refusing, but I do know that it isn't because you don't want me. If it's Rowena, forget it. For all I know she and Chris haven't even gone to the opera, they may be at some party together. It doesn't matter to me, and this wouldn't matter to her.'

'It isn't Rowena,' Harriet assured him. 'After James I'm not very keen on getting involved with anyone on a regular basis.'

'But we're good together,' he protested, deciding that whatever else happened he wasn't going to pass this scene on to Mark; it was too humiliating ever to repeat aloud.

Harriet decided that she'd kept him waiting long enough, and he was certainly sufficiently unsettled to think twice before he took her compliance for granted again. 'Well, perhaps a bath would be nice,' she conceded. 'Usually I take showers.'

Lewis was amazed by the wave of relief that washed over him. His heart was beating rapidly and it took all of his self-control not to simply take Harriet there and then on the floor of the drawing-room.

Instead, pausing only to collect a bottle of chilled

Chardonnay and two glasses, he led her upstairs to Rowena's bathroom and there filled the tub with water, adding plenty of erotic Japanese sandalwood oil which engulfed the room with its subtly arousing fragrance.

Slowly he undressed Harriet, then let her undress him, and all the time he kept touching and kissing her, whispering in her ear exactly what he proposed to do during their time together.

He sat her between his outspread legs with her back to him and the warm water came up to her breasts. Tenderly he soaped her along her spine using long featherlight strokes. Harriet felt herself dissolving beneath his touch and when he laid her back in the water so that her head was against his chest she expected him to move on to her breasts, which were tight and aching, but instead he washed her arms, ending with the hands which he lingered over, teasing every finger until the rest of her body was screaming for attention.

It seemed an eternity before his hands picked up the soap and he lathered it over her stomach, causing the muscles to leap and jump in a dance of their own. Once he brushed her breasts, but it was such a faint caress that she could almost have imagined it and it served only to increase the aching sensation behind each nipple.

After that he got her to move so that she was on all fours with her head at the tap end of the bath. Then she had to raise her buttocks high above the water. He proceeded to cover the cheeks of her bottom with the suds before lightly running a finger between them. The slight tickling of the bubbles was incredibly arousing, and when he washed them off with bathwater she wanted to ask him to do it again, but Lewis had other plans.

He turned her over again and this time crouched above her, straddling her body in the water until at last his hands were washing each of her breasts in turn, taking particular care over the nipples, which he covered in suds until they vanished from sight.

Again the bubbles burst, tickling the tender flesh and causing her breasts to harden and the veins to become visible. Lewis smiled at her, then took a sponge and held it high above her before squeezing the contents out in a steady stream over her nipples.

Harriet gave a gasp of pleasure and Lewis repeated the procedure, this time holding the sponge above the soapy breasts for even longer until she was begging him to let the water cascade down.

He had intended letting her wash him, but their love play had aroused him more than he'd anticipated and he didn't want to wait any longer before possessing her.

Pushing her soapy hands gently off him he climbed out of the bath. 'I'll take my turn another time,' he promised. He then wrapped her in a warm towel, picked her up and carried her out of the bathroom, through Rowena's room and into his own. Once he'd laid her on his bed he went back to the bathroom for the wine and together they drank from opposite sides of the same glass, stopping now and again to exchange kisses and let the crisp refreshing liquid pass from one mouth to the other.

They were both frantic for each other now, but Harriet had already discovered the joys of delaying the ultimate pleasure and it was she who got Lewis to lie on his stomach so that she could pour some of the wine on to the top of his spine.

His body jerked at the unexpected coldness, then as it trickled across each vertebra he felt her soft warm tongue licking at it. Her tongue and the wine were an incredible contrast to each other. This time he was the one to writhe against the duvet, and Harriet watched his movements with fascination.

'Keep still,' she told him, remembering her own struggles to control her body, and beneath her Lewis stiffened, then forced himself to obey, fascinated by this change in the balance of power.

After working down his spine with her tongue, Harriet dipped her middle finger in the wine and then eased it between the cheeks of his bottom, stopping every time he gave an involuntary jerk.

For Lewis it was the most delicious torment as he tried to quell his excitement sufficiently for her finger to reach its ultimate goal. She refused to let him hurry her, or to move except when he was still, but eventually the tip of the finger touched his prostate gland and he felt his already hard erection swell. The pressure in his tightly drawn up testicles seemed unbearable.

When her finger caressed the gland again he had to move to stop himself from coming. 'Harriet, stop! I can't take any more,' he murmured, and she felt a surge of triumph as she withdrew her teasing digit and let him roll onto his back.

Lewis saw Harriet looking down at him and for the first time since their affair had begun he reached his hands up, pulled her face down and kissed her long and deeply on the mouth. His tongue teased the insides of her soft lips and then flicked round her teeth before easing its way between them. Her own tongue responded, and she licked the corners of his mouth before the tempo of the kiss increased and he started to thrust his tongue deeper into her mouth, duplicating the urgent thrusting of his erection.

They were lying locked together now, Harriet on top of him, revelling in the feel of his muscular body beneath her, and when he rolled her on to her side so that they were face-to-face she stared deeply into his eyes, trying to read something from their expression.

Lewis stared back. His breathing was still rapid and his hands unable to leave her alone as they moved down her side, over her hipbone and down the slender flank. His penis strained against her lower abdomen and he moved down the bed so that he could use it to caress her clitoris with tiny teasing movements, then watched as her eyes darkened and the pupils enlarged with her growing excitement.

Harriet began to wriggle with impatience, suddenly no longer concerned with whether or not she could see any true emotion in his eyes. All she wanted was to have him inside her, to be filled yet again in order to satisfy the craving that he had aroused in her.

Lewis was lying on his left side and he raised Harriet's left leg over his waist then slid deep into her, his hands clasped round her buttocks. For a moment they both stayed motionless, each of them savouring their body's sensations, and then Lewis moved.

He withdrew to the entrance of her vagina, tantalised her frantic flesh for a few seconds, then pulled hard on her buttocks so that she was propelled on to him and he re-entered her in a rush.

The angle of penetration was perfect for Harriet because every time he withdrew and then pulled her back to him all the nerve endings around her clitoris were stimulated and the tense tightness that she'd come to associate with their love-making filled her pelvic area, spreading slowly upwards in darting streaks.

When the tempo of his thrusting increased, Harriet lost all control of herself. Her only thought was for the pleasure he brought her and she gave herself over to it utterly. Her tiny cries and whimpers stimulated Lewis more than any wild thrashing would have done and when she finally took up the rhythm he'd started for herself, moving her own body against his at the pace they both wanted, he let one of his hands move between the cheeks of her bottom and inserted a finger into her rear.

He moved it very slowly, just sufficiently to allow him to press firmly against the walls of her rectum and as Harriet's body gathered itself together for the final explosion of excitement the delicate nerve endings deep within her were stimulated and the pressure travelled through to her front so that all sensations were doubled.

Lewis felt her body arching against him, heard her moan of delight and then she was twisting and turning, almost jerking away from him in the mindless spasms of her climax. Aroused to incredible heights himself he caught hold of her body and roughly pulled her back against him, his penis now so tight and swollen that he could feel the sides of her vaginal walls pulsating around him and with a shout he spilled himself into her warm velvet softness.

As Harriet's body started to recover from her orgasm she realised that there was still a soft but undeniable pulse beating between her thighs. She tried to keep still, ashamed to think that her body might be demanding yet more satisfaction.

Lewis lay quietly, his erection subsiding within her,

but watching her closely he knew from the expression in her eyes and the almost imperceptible movements of her hips that she was capable of more.

He was pleased. This was what he'd hoped for. A woman who would become more and more capable of sexual arousal. A woman whose body would take over from her mind so that in the end she would do anything for the satisfaction he had taught her to need.

'You'd like more, wouldn't you?' he whispered.

Harriet shook her head, still denying her own sexuality.

'There's no reason to be ashamed,' he assured her. 'It's a compliment to me.'

'But I've never been like this,' protested Harriet, remembering how relieved she always was when James had finished.

'This is a new life. You can be quite different here,' he murmured and with relief she felt one of his hands pressing against her lower belly just above the pubic bone, exactly where she always ached when need for release started to build in her.

His hand moved in circles, the pressure increasing as Harriet's body responded. Suddenly she felt a new sensation, a strange heaviness buried so deep inside her it was impossible to be sure where it began, and sharp sensations like currents of electricity speared through her from below her clitoris up to where his hand was moving relentlessly.

Lewis knew exactly what was happening. He was arousing not only the nerve endings from the clitoris but also those leading from the bladder and the combination lead, for some women, to their most intense orgasms.

Harriet seemed likely to be one of those women because she began to cry out, and her eyes were enormous as she looked up at him. 'Don't stop!' she begged when his hand was briefly still. 'It feels incredible.'

'You like it?'

Harriet bit on her lip as his hand dug deeper and the hot, tingling pressure intensified. 'Yes,' she assured him, although now the sensation was so intense that she wasn't quite sure it could be pleasure.

Her body knew better than she did, and began to swell until the skin of her abdomen felt too tight. Moaning she tried to move, to slow down the mounting sensations that threatened to overwhelm her. Lewis simply let the fingers of his hand part the top of her outer lips, and while he continued to press firmly against her lower belly he also teased the sides of her pulsating bud, never staying in one place for more than a few seconds but all the time moving so that her flesh jumped and the throbbing between her legs seemed to be echoed by the sound of her pulse drumming in her ears.

Lewis's own erection had now subsided but at the sight of Harriet being aroused to new and only dimly understood heights, he felt himself start to stir again.

As the startling feelings continued to grow, Harriet's breasts began to ache and after only a slight hesitation she reached up, drawing Lewis's head down towards her.

'Tell me what you want,' he murmured.

'My breasts,' she moaned, thrusting them up towards his mouth. 'They ache.'

'And what do you want me to do about it?' he teased.

Harriet didn't know if she could tell him, but the insistent clamouring of her needy flesh won over her deeply ingrained reticence at vocalising her desires. 'Suck them for me, Lewis, please.'

'Hard or soft?' he asked, his hand still continuing its pressing movements and his finger drawing up the clitoral hood as he worked so that he could brush lightly across the top of the exposed nub.

'Hard!' she begged, her body now nothing but a pressurised aching need for the final stimuation that would allow her another crescendo of pleasure.

He smiled and then his mouth closed around one of her hard nipples and he was sucking steadily. The pressure grew, just as the pressure on her clitoris and the over-excited nerves from her bladder grew and with this final touch the flashes and the streaks of bliss that were searing through her at last came together and she was wracked by almost painfully fierce muscular contractions that seemed to turn her whole body into hot liquid as it tumbled into total satisfaction.

Somewhere in the distance Harriet heard a strange keening sound, little realising that it was her own cry of ecstasy, and as her back arched and her upper torso twisted and turned Lewis let his teeth graze the very tip of the nipple in his mouth and he continued stimulating her clitoris until the final tiny muscular tremors had died away and she was at last still.

For Harriet, covered in a thin sheen of perspiration, her limbs almost weightless, it had been the best moment yet and she closed her eyes to try and recall exactly how it had felt at the final moment when her orgasm swept over her. She could remember the earlier sensations, the strange sharp pressure, the aching nipple and the feeling of Lewis's mouth covering it, but those last glorious moments eluded her. They were impossible to recreate by memory.

When she, opened her eyes Lewis was propped up on one elbow, watching her with an expression of tenderness. 'Do you want any more?' he asked with a smile.

Harriet shook her head. 'That was out of this world. I never thought . . . I wouldn't have believed it possible to feel so much.'

'Believe me there's still plenty more for you to discover, but not tonight, I think!' He kissed her gently on the forehead, his hands stroking the sides of her neck. 'I really should go and do some work. Will you be all right on your own?'

'I can't stay here,' said Harriet quickly. 'I must get back to my own room.'

'Nonsense,' said Lewis easily. 'Rowena won't look in here tonight, and you'll be up long before her in the morning. Besides, when I do come to bed I want you to be here for me. I'd like to spend the night next to you.'

Unexpectedly touched, Harriet sighed voluptuously

and gave in. He must know what he was doing, and anyway she felt too tired to go down to the first floor. The prospect of a cold bed was distinctly unappealing as well. 'All right,' she conceded and with a final kiss Lewis left her.

'Why do I have to keep coming out at night?' asked Mark irritably.

'My best ideas come to me then,' replied Lewis smoothly.

'I haven't finished the last part you gave me yet.'

'As long as it's out of my head and into yours that's all that interests me. I've decided to add a complication.'

'You mean the film isn't complex enough?' asked Mark incredulously.

'The idea is, but the relationships were too cut and dried. I want the hero to start feeling something for the secretary.'

'Love?'

Lewis shook his head. 'No, not love, but something more than he'd intended. She has to matter as a person, not just as a catalyst. He brought her in to try and get his wife back, now he finds himself feeling tenderness or compassion towards her.'

'Why?' asked Mark, wondering who was going to play the hero. Good looks and virility were easy enough; deeper emotions often eluded the stars who were best at the surface charm.

'Because she's special. She's got to have something that draws him to her. It can't be beauty – after all the heroine has that in abundance. Let's say a certain unpredictability, plus intelligence.'

'You mean she's moody?'

Lewis struggled to keep his temper in check. 'No, moody women are not enchanting in life or on film. I thought she might start being a little remote, succumb less easily to the hero's seductions. When he has to work harder he finds her more interesting.'

Mark sighed and started to scribble notes.

'Why the sighing?' asked Lewis.

'You know what they say about film treatments – you should be able to sum up the basic idea in one sentence. I'd like to see you do that with this story.'

'None of my films have conformed, but it hasn't stopped them succeeding.'

'I'm not saying this won't be a great film, just that you're breaking all the rules.'

'I certainly am,' retorted Lewis.

At that moment Rowena put her head round the door. 'Heavens, still working, Lewis? And what are you doing here at this hour, Mark?'

'I called him over. How was *Rigoletto?*'

'It was *Attila* and it was great. For once the acting was good too.'

'I'll take your word for it.'

'Will you be long?' asked Rowena, and Lewis knew by the look in her eyes what she meant.

'I'm not sure,' he said carefully, but he made sure he gave her a warm smile before turning his attention back to Mark.

'Try not to be,' murmured Rowena, closing the door softly behind her.

Mark, who still thought Rowena was the sexiest woman he'd ever met, glanced at Lewis. 'Do you want to leave it there?'

'Just read it back to me,' said Lewis. 'I want to be sure you've got it right.' As Mark read back his notes, Lewis tried to picture what was going on upstairs.

Rowena, encouraged by her husband's warm glance and feeling aroused after the excitement of the opera and a long, lingering meal with Chris, had decided that she'd wait for Lewis in his room. Chris would be expecting her, but tonight she wanted Lewis. She wanted to be in control, to play the sex goddess. It was never like that with Chris. He'd known her for too long and understood her too well for it to be possible.

She didn't bother to change her clothes. Lewis enjoyed undressing her and frequently chose to leave some of her underwear on while he took her, finding the sight of the soft silks and satins with their hand-made lace edging against her skin arousing.

Walking along the top landing she opened the door into his bedroom and was halfway towards the bed before she realised that it was already occupied. With a quickly smothered sound of surprise she stood look-ing at the sleeping Harriet.

Exhausted, Harriet had fallen asleep on her back, totally naked, and was lying with her limbs sprawled out over the duvet. Her normally smooth hair was rum-pled and her skin shone with what Rowena recognised as the glow of total sexual satisfaction.

For a long time the film star stood there, studying the naked woman, realising that while she and Chris had been dining together, exciting each other with tales of what they would do with Harriet when she'd been drawn into their sexual games, Lewis had yet again been making love to her.

Remembering how the younger woman had looked the first time she'd been to bed with Lewis, Rowena wondered what she looked like now. She wondered if her body was more adventurous, if she played a more active role, and as her thoughts took off in that direction she found herself becoming even more aroused.

She was so lost in her thoughts that she never heard Lewis come in – it was only when he put a hand over her mouth from behind that she realised he was there. 'What were you thinking?' he whispered softly.

'I was wondering what she'd been like tonight?' Rowena whispered back.

'Magnificent. Do you want to touch her?'

She frowned. 'Surely she'd never let me.'

'She won't know,' Lewis promised her, keeping his voice low. Rowena watched him draw a black velvet mask from his pocket, then he sat on the bed beside the sleeping Harriet and carefully slipped it over her head until her eyes were covered. Exhausted, Harriet slumbered on.

'Touch her,' breathed Lewis against Rowena's ear.

'Touch her breasts, they're very responsive. If she wakes, I'll speak.'

'She'll know it isn't you.' Rowena's protest was only half-hearted. The prospect of touching the unknowing girl, of stirring her senses back to life, was deliciously exciting.

'She's very tired,' Lewis assured her. 'Her mind won't function that well, and she certainly won't be expecting it to be anyone but me touching her.

Rowena licked the tip of her right forefinger and then crept close to the bed. As Lewis sat at Harriet's head, Rowena sat halfway down the bed and then leant over the prone figure to draw a damp teasing circle round Harriet's right nipple. Harriet made a small sound of pleasure in her sleep and the nipple began to swell. Rowena glanced at her husband but he was watching Harriet's reaction. Encouraged, Rowena slid her fingertip round the areola and watched the ring of flesh expand.

In her dreams Harriet was lying on a grassy bank and Lewis was touching her breast which was exposed to the warm summer air. She moved a little, trying to get him to touch the other breast and to her delight he did. This time the touch was firmer, and then suddenly her nipple was pinched very lightly between his finger-tips and this increase in sensation began to draw her out of her sleep.

Rowena smiled at the sight of the recently pinched nipple standing so proudly erect. She let her hand trace a delicate pattern round the circumference of the breast and then at a sign from Lewis bent her head and caressed it with her lips.

Harriet's eyes opened slowly. She was aware now that it wasn't a dream, that Lewis really was touching her breasts, but to her shock she couldn't see anything and she struggled to sit up.

Rowena quickly drew back, anxious not to betray her presence, while Lewis wrapped his arms round Harriet's shoulders. 'It's all right,' he soothed her. 'I've put a mask on you; it increases the intensity of the sensation.'

'I'm tired,' Harriet murmured.

'Then let me do all the work,' said Lewis, laying her back against the pillows.

Harriet waited. Her breasts felt cool now that the saliva was evaporating but suddenly she felt something warm being spread across her belly and inner thighs. It felt like a lotion, and was too thick for oil.

'What's that?' she demanded.

'Something very special,' said Lewis, watching his titian-haired wife spreading the gel over his mistress's body. 'You'll love it.' She did like it, liked the tingling warmth of it, the way her blood began to course more quickly through her veins, and she felt herself moistening between her thighs.

Lewis was careful not to keep his arms round Harriet while Rowena worked, knowing that even in her half-sleeping state she could realise that there were too many hands on her. When Rowena started to blow on the gel he pressed his hands on Harriet's shoulders, aware that what followed would have her twisting and turning and afraid of contact between the two women.

Rowena had often used the gel before, and she too knew how the soft warmth of its application increased to a fiery glow almost more than the body could take, and she watched the way Harriet's belly began to tighten and heard with amusement the low guttural sound deep in her throat.

For Harriet the stimulation was unexpected and not entirely to her liking. She twisted her lower body around on the bed, hoping for some relief from the strange burning that was permeating her flesh but movement only increased the effect of the gel and she began to make protesting sounds.

'Wait,' said Lewis. 'It gets better.'

He released Harriet who sat upright but stayed on the bed because of the mask. Rowena went into the bathroom and soaked a hand towel in cold water. She returned and Lewis told Harriet to lie down again, promising that now she'd start to enjoy what he was doing to her.

Harriet trusted him, their tender lovemaking of earlier in the evening had increased the depth of her feelings for him and the last thing she wanted to do now was give him any hint that she might not appreciate his more sophisticated games and so she went along with what he wanted.

The shock of the ice-cold towel being laid across her overheated belly made her cry out despite herself and then the towel was wrapped tightly beneath her sides. Lewis did this, knowing that the size of his hands would be felt, which should reassure her if any reassurance was needed.

Rowena waited until the cold towel was in place, and then as Harriet's nerve endings started to spark with the contrast of hot and cold, the film star slid her finger, still covered with some of the heat-inducing gel, inside the other woman's vagina.

Lewis reached out to stop her, but he was too late and suddenly Harriet was writhing uncontrollably, her legs jerking and her hips twisting as the stimulating gel spread warmth through her delicate internal tissue.

She was literally on fire for him now. Aroused beyond bearing by what Rowena had done, Harriet's body couldn't keep still and she heard herself crying out for Lewis to help her, to bring her to the climax that the gel had initiated but was unable to satisfy.

Rowena watched her PA as she begged Lewis to do something to help her climax, to touch her on her aching needy clitoris, and her own heart raced at the eroticism of the scene and the knowledge that she had been responsible for bringing Harriet to this state of abandonment.

Lewis watched Harriet's straining body and knew that she would need something special to assuage the burning desire Rowena had aroused in her. Murmuring reassurances to his mistress he slipped out of his clothes and his eyes flicked towards the massage oil standing on his dressing table. Rowena understood what he meant and tiptoed to fetch it. Pouring it into her right hand she lavishly oiled his belly and thighs before letting her hands slide over his straining penis and testicles.

She oiled him cleverly, easing the lubrication around the rim of the glans, a movement which she knew he loved and which caused the glans to turn an even deeper shade of purple as his excitement grew.

Harriet was still moaning, calling Lewis's name and trying to reach for him. Lewis had to turn away from his wife's ministrations before she caused him to ejaculate. Rowena felt a pang of disappointment when he moved but consoled herself with the thought that she would be able to watch him attempting to satisfy the desperate Harriet.

As Lewis turned Harriet on to her face she struggled against him. 'I just want you inside me!' she protested. 'I don't need any more stimulation.' He ignored her, and when he slid the oiled lower half of his body backwards and forwards across her thighs and buttocks she caught her breath in surprise.

It was a wonderful sensation. His hard smooth body slipped to and fro in a gentle flowing movement and the stimulation was delicate yet intense. When he moved low on her his penis slipped between her parted legs and she felt it brush against her hungry sex.

At last he penetrated her, but so slowly that at first she couldn't believe that was what he was doing. Then she realised that each penetration coincided with an upward glide of his body and all the time his hand was massaging her shoulders and the back of her neck.

Each liquid penetration eased the dreadful sensation of fiery need that had filled her and instead it was as though she was melting with the bliss of the contact.

When he turned her on to her back again she didn't make any protest because she was now lost in the exquisite gliding movements of their dance of love. Gently he pressed her knees towards her breasts, at the same time sliding his oiled penis back into her.

Harriet's body felt ripe and lush to her, as though her whole being was changing because of what he was doing. She wanted it to go on forever.

Lewis started to rock his pelvis in slow rhythmic movements which aroused every nerve ending within her, and those nerve endings – already brought to fever pitch by Rowena's gel – sent frantic messages to her brain that made her muscles coil and ripple, then start to tense as her climax began to approach. She could

feel it building higher and higher and thrust against
Lewis in an attempt to hurry the final explosion along,
but he slowed her with hands and soft whispers. When
she continued to move, he stopped and only began
again once she was still.

From the end of the bed Rowena watched in trembling excitement. She'd never imagined Harriet capable
of such passion. The sight of the other woman's
swollen straining body, of seeing her own husband
glide over another woman in practised movements, all
made her long for a climax of her own and without
realising it she slipped her hand inside her blouse and
started to fondle her breasts, pinching the already tight
nipples between her fingers.

Finally Harriet's body could wait no longer. Despite
her own lack of movement, despite Lewis urging her to
delay just a little longer, the pleasure started on its final
upward spiral and her head moved restlessly against the
pillows while a delicate pink flush of arousal suffused
her neck and breasts.

Finally Lewis allowed his pace to increase and his
hips moved faster. Harriet stared into the midnight
blackness caused by the mask and felt her entire body
gather in on itself before seeming to shatter into a

thousand pieces. Bright lights exploded behind her eyelids as her body was finally allowed to come.

'There, wasn't that good?' whispered Lewis against her ear.

Exhausted, Harriet could only murmur something unintelligible and then she fell back to sleep, a sleep from which Lewis and Rowena had already aroused her once that night.

When he was certain she was asleep. Lewis left Harriet and walked across to his wife. He removed her hands from inside her blouse and smiled into her feverishly bright eyes. 'Perhaps you'd better pay Chris a visit,' he suggested. 'I'm sure he was expecting you anyway.'

'I want you,' said Rowena, winding herself around him like a cat.

He pushed her firmly away. 'Not tonight, Rowena. Tonight belongs to Harriet. Be grateful you were allowed to watch. It wasn't meant to happen yet.'

'She'll never know. Take me here!' urged Rowena, but Lewis refused and drew her out of his bedroom. He was well satisfied with the night's events.

Chapter Seven

FOR THE NEXT two nights Lewis spent hours in either Harriet's or his own room, bringing her time and again to the heights of ecstasy she had come to expect from him, and every time she climaxed, every time he taught her something new, she was bound more closely to him. The fact that he was slowly being bound more closely to her was something Lewis chose to ignore. Then, on the Saturday, everything changed.

Harriet had been surprised to be invited to the dinner party, and had cancelled her planned evening with Ella because she didn't want to miss the chance of a genuine film star's party. Ella green with envy, had understood but demanded a full report in exchange for being let down.

'I want to hear all about what Rowena wore, ate, drank and how she behaved,' she told Harriet.

'Of course. I'll tell you about Lewis too.'

'I'm sure you will,' said Ella, who already had her suspicions about Harriet and the star's husband.

When they finally sat down to dinner, Harriet found that she was seated next to a man called Mark who told her he was a scripwriter.

'Have you worked on any big films?' asked Harriet politely, keeping a careful eye on Lewis who was deep in animated conversation with a beautiful Eurasian girl.

'Both of Lewis's Oscar-winning hits. Not that they were the same kind of film as his next one, but the script was important. You can't always rely on images to tell the whole story for you.'

'I suppose not,' said Harriet vaguely.

'What do you do?' enquired Mark, who thought she was a most unlikely dinner guest for Lewis and Rowena. She was very attractive, but didn't seem to have any idea about the film industry.

'I'm Rowena's personal assistant,' said Harriet. 'She's hired me for the time she's over here. Sometimes I do work for Lewis as well.'

Mark stared at Harriet with a new found interest.

'You mean, Rowena's really taken on an attractive secretary?'

Harriet laughed. 'I'm certainly a secretary! Why the surprise?'

Mark struggled to regain his composure. He couldn't believe that he was thinking along the right lines. Surely even Lewis wouldn't go to such extreme lengths in order to get the film right, but then again Lewis was known as a man who'd do anything for his art.

'I supposed I expected her to have someone middle-aged and frumpy. Fragile ego, that sort of thing, you know how film stars are!' he said lightly.

'Actually I don't,' responded Harriet. 'I've never had anything to do with films before, but I do admire Lewis a lot. He's so well balanced.' She glanced down the table at him as she spoke, and Mark could tell by the stiffening of her body that Lewis's clear interest in the Eurasian girl upset her.

'Are you engaged, married or fancy free?' he asked casually, trying to find a way of confirming his growing suspicion about Harriet's real role in the household, while at the same time hoping for her sake that he was wrong.

She laughed. 'Entirely fancy free! I was engaged, but

ended it just before I came to work here. This has been a new start for me.'

'And you like it?' queried Mark.

Harriet couldn't help another fleeting look at Lewis. 'Yes, it's the best job I've ever had.'

'You don't find Rowena too demanding?'

'Actually she's been very kind. Quite often she's busy helping Chris go through scripts and things like that, so once I've finished her work I type out letters for Lewis. If he hasn't anything for me then I'm free to do what I like.'

At the memory of what that frequently entailed, Harriet's cheeks were stained a delicate pink and Mark knew then with absolute certainty that he was right. Incredible as it seemed, Lewis was actually playing out his film in his own home. This explained the strange changes in script direction, the sudden alterations in the balance of power. It wasn't that Lewis was having midnight brain storms, the man was simply telling Mark things that had happened.

The scriptwriter stared at Harriet through new eyes. If she was really having an affair with Lewis then Rowena must know about it. Not only that but as far as he could remember there had been a time when

Harriet must have caught Rowena and Lewis making love in his study. Looking at her it was hard to believe she would allow herself to be caught up in any kind of sexual triangle, but as he was well aware looks could be deceptive.

For a moment he felt like warning Harriet. She was clearly in love with Lewis, not simply having a good time with him, and although she thought she was in competition with Rowena there was no way she could ever guess the true complexity of the game she was so innocently playing.

'Harriet,' he said tentatively.

She smiled at him. 'Yes?'

'Do you think this is really the right job for you?' he blurted out.

Stunned, Harriet stared at him in silence, trying to understand what he was saying.

'They're very sophisticated people,' Mark blundered on. 'If you ever want to get away, to . . .'

'I'm not a prisoner,' protested Harriet, her voice rising with indignation. 'I'm free to leave whenever I like.'

Lewis couldn't hear Harriet's words but he could hear her voice and knew by the tone that something

Mark had said had made her anxious. He looked down the table at his scriptwriter and his eyes were dark. 'Something wrong?' he asked politely.

Mark shook his head. 'Of course not.'

'Harriet?'

She smiled at Lewis. 'No, nothing's wrong. Mark was just warning me about the perils of working for people like you!'

'If he thinks it's that perilous he'd better find himself a new employer,' said Lewis. He kept his voice light but Mark felt a chill run through him. Lewis was ruthless, and if he thought for one moment that Mark was endangering his work then he would instantly have him removed and sent back to the States. The two previous Oscars, their years of collaboration, would count for nothing.

'Luckily Harriet's far too sensible to listen to me,' Mark retorted. 'I was only trying to prise her away so that she could work for me. I'm in desperate need of a good secretary myself.'

'Harriet's far more than a secreatary,' said Rowena, breaking off her conversation with one of the film's financial backers. 'Why, she's really one of the family now – isn't that right, Harriet?'

Out of the blue Harriet remembered the feel of hands on her body a few nights earlier. Hands that had given her such pleasure when she'd been half-asleep and masked. She looked at Rowena's hands, wondering why she should think of that at this moment when Rowena hadn't even been there. Guilt, she supposed.

'Harriet?' repeated Rowena.

She managed a warm smile. 'It's very kind of you to say so, Rowena.'

Rowena's best professional bubbly laugh sounded round the room. 'So modest – it's a wonderful English virtue, I find! Why, Harriet's charmed us all. My husband, my brother Chris, and me too of course. None of us can imagine how things were before she joined us, isn't that true, Lew?'

Lewis, realising that his wife had probably had too much to drink, attempted to change the direction of the conversation. 'Quite true, darling. I've never seen your filing in such good order! The tomato and olive tart was superb – you must congratulate the cook.'

'I think Harriet should do some work for me,' said Chris suddenly.

Harriet turned her head towards him. 'I'd be glad to, as long as I wasn't needed by Rowena or Lewis.'

Chris, his face flushed by wine, laughed heartily. 'You could spare her occasionally, couldn't you, Rowena?'

Rowena's lips tightened. 'I hardly think you need a secretary to read scripts for you, Chris, and you certainly don't have fan mail to deal with.'

All round the table people fell silent. It was common knowledge that Rowena and Chris were devoted to each other, so this sudden sharpness and the deliberate put-down were totally unexpected.

Chris didn't look taken aback though, he merely smiled his most charming smile. 'Perhaps that would change if I wasn't forever living in your shadow, Rowena. Now that your days as a sex goddess are over it might be my turn to carry on the family tradition. I'd love to play a handsome seducer.'

'Rowena's days as a sex goddess are only "over", as you put it, because she wants to be taken seriously as an actress,' said Lewis quickly. 'I'm sure we can all see tonight that the choice must have been hers.'

'Absolutely,' said Mark, quick to pick up a cue.

Rowena smiled at both men, ignoring her half-brother. 'How sweet of you, Lewis, and you too, Mark. Goodness, is that the time? Does anyone want any more cheese or shall we ladies withdraw?'

Dark Secret

The tiny goats' cheeses wrapped in vine leaves had been delicious, as had the strawberry sorbet before them, but Harriet had tasted very little, and it was with some relief that she went with the other women into the drawing-room. Despite her denial, Mark's words had unsettled her, and so had Lewis's admiration of his companion at the dinner table.

Although her fame had come through her ability to portray great sexual magnetism on the screen, Rowena was unusual in so far as she had always been able to gain the admiration of women as well. Tonight, laughing and chatting with the other female guests, she wove her spell over them all and Harriet noticed the way even the Eurasian girl's beauty and youth seemed to dim in Rowena's presence.

Briefly she wondered how she could ever hope to capture Lewis's heart, but then she told herself that whatever her hold over him, Rowena certainly didn't have his heart, in which case Harriet had as much chance as anyone of winning it.

Later the men joined them and the conversation became noisier while the air grew thick with cigar smoke. After a time Harriet felt she'd suffocate if she didn't get any air and she made her way outside.

She went to the walled garden at the bottom of the sloping lawn and sat down on the carved wooden seat, drawing in deep breaths of the mild summer night air.

When she heard someone approaching her heart began to beat faster. She was sure that it was Lewis, that he'd followed her outside to make arrangements for when the guests had gone, and her body tingled with excited anticipation. 'I thought I saw you leave,' said a voice, but it didn't belong to Lewis, it belonged to Chris.

'It was stuffy in there,' explained Harriet, struggling to keep the disappointment out of her voice. 'I hope Rowena won't think me rude.'

'She won't notice you've gone!' laughed Chris. 'When Rowena's centre stage she doesn't keep a head count of the admiring audience. As long as there are plenty of people she's satisfied.'

'I think you're being unfair to her,' retorted Harriet. 'She isn't nearly as vain as I'd expected her to be.'

'And you're far more beautiful than I'd expected you to be,' murmured Chris, sitting down next to her.

Harriet moved her legs slightly so that her knees weren't touching his. She didn't like his intimate tone, and she couldn't help remembering how she'd seen him behaving with Rowena in the film star's bedroom. The strange sick excitement she'd felt then was still stirred at the memory, but it made her want Lewis, not Chris.

'Have you always been beautiful?' Chris asked, resting an arm along the back of the seat.

Harriet felt like laughing, but there was something about him that made the idea seem a dangerous one so she attempted to brush the remark aside in another way. 'Yes, from the moment I was born. Nurses swooned away and one of the doctors asked my mother if he could come and ask for my hand eighteen years on.'

'You really are beautiful,' said Chris. 'Surely you know that?'

'I think you've drunk too much wine,' said Harriet. 'Rowena's beautiful, I'm attractive. There's a big difference.'

He put a hand on her knee and she froze into stillness. 'Rowena's a witch,' he confided. 'She traps people with her beauty and then they can't get free. You wouldn't do that, would you?'

'I've no idea. I haven't managed to trap anyone yet.'

'It's no joke, being trapped,' he continued, his voice

verging on self-pity. 'You end up despising yourself for your weakness, but it doesn't make any difference.'

Harriet knew she had to pretend that she wasn't aware of Chris's intimate reltionship with Rowena. 'You're only her half-brother!' she protested. 'If you got married, made a life for yourself, you'd be free straight away. Why hang around here if she makes you miserable?'

'Because I need her,' he said fiercely. 'We need each other. Sometimes I think we'll only be free when one of us is dead.'

His hand tightened on her knee and she edged further away from him. At once the arm along the back of the seat grabbed her round her shoulders. 'Don't you know what an obsession's like?' he demanded. 'Haven't you ever been consumed with need for someone?'

Yes, thought Harriet, I'm consumed with need for Lewis right now but even if he wants to come and see me he can't because you're sitting here preventing him. 'No,' she said calmly.

'I think that's a lie,' said Chris softly, and then she felt the hand on her left shoulder start to edge up the side of her neck in an undeniably intimate gesture.

Harriet jumped to her feet. 'I'd better go back now.'

'Why?' he asked sulkily.

'I feel better, that's why.'

'Lewis won't have missed you; he's busy with Marita. She's stunning, don't you think? And Lewis's type as well.'

'Really?'

'Oh yes, Lewis likes women like that. She's quite without emotion you see. All Marita wants is to get on in films, and she's beautiful enough to manage it. You can still sleep your way to a reasonable amount of success, but Lewis will sleep with her and not use her in any film. He dislikes emotional commitment, you see.'

'He married Rowena,' Harriet pointed out, longing to get back to the house and see if what Chris was saying was true.

'He married her and he scares her but he sure as hell isn't in love with her,' snarled Chris. 'If he was he'd try to satisfy her more.'

'I don't think you should be talking to me like this,' protested Harriet.

Chris stood up and grabbed her by an arm, twisting her round to face him. 'Why not? You're being screwed by Lewis, aren't you? Surely that puts you on an equal footing with Rowena, and I often discuss Lewis's failings as a husband with her.'

'If you don't let go of me,' said Harriet fiercely, 'I shall slap your face and shout for help.'

For a moment Chris hesitated, but then his hand dropped to his side and he sank back on the seat again. 'Run back to Lewis,' he jeered, 'but don't blame me when you find he's no longer interested. He has the attention span of a two-year-old where women are concerned. No doubt he had a great time with you, but that time's over now.'

'You're drunk and I don't want to hear another word,' snapped Harriet, and then she was running away from him, back up the lawn towards the crowded house.

While she'd been gone some of the dinner guests had paired off and were engaged in acts of varying intimacy in the hall, the drawing-room and even on the stairs. Rowena was sitting in the conservatory drinking coffee and talking to another woman but there was no sign of Lewis, or the Eurasian girl, Marita.

'I'm off to bed,' Harriet told Rowena. 'It was a lovely evening.'

Rowena peered at her through the smoke of one of

her rare cigarettes. 'Did you enjoy it? You don't look very happy.'

'I'm just tired. I'm not used to such late hours!'

'Have you seen my brother?'

'Chris went into the garden,' Harriet told her.

Rowena smiled. 'He's drunk too much. I'll say good-night to Lewis for you; he's busy right now.'

The woman with her laughed. 'He certainly is. Marita keeps most men busy. She nearly killed my husband last year!' Rowena's laughter joined her friend's and Harriet fled upstairs, certain that they were secretly mocking her.

She lay awake until six in the morning but Lewis didn't join her, and she guessed then that the story must have been true and Marita had kept him busy. At first she wept, but then she told herself that crying was useless. A man like that was bound to be used to casual affairs – what she had to do was make herself indispensable to him, no matter what was necessary to achieve it.

As Harriet finally fell asleep, Lewis disengaged himself from the smooth golden limbs of his companion and lay on his back wondering why it was that despite Marita's athleticism and incredible skill at fellatio she had failed to hold his attention. Once or twice he'd found himself thinking about Harriet, picturing her in the Eurasian girl's place. It was all very unsettling and most unlike him.

In the end he woke Marita, handed her her clothes and sent her home in his car. He didn't want any more to do with her, and knew by the expression on her face that she wouldn't want anything to do with him again. It was of no importance. It had only ever been intended as a moment's pleasure and a spur to what was intended to be Harriet's increasing need for him now that he was going to leave her alone for a time. The realisation that he wouldn't be sleeping with her for nearly a week hurt. She was meant to miss him but he hadn't anticipated missing her as well.

No one appeared downstairs in the house the following morning until twelve o' clock, and even then it was only Harriet. She made herself toast and coffee then took it into the sun-drenched conservatory. She wanted to see Lewis, to speak to him, and her body ached for his skilled touch but she wasn't sure what she was going to say when he did come down.

He and Rowena eventually joined her a little after two in the afternoon, and much to her surprise the pair of them seemed thoroughly absorbed in each other. Just as he had when Harriet first arrived at the house, Lewis kept touching his wife. His hands would caress her back and shoulders, or he would touch her on the arm to emphasise a point in his conversation. They both looked cheerful and were friendly towards Harriet but she felt herself being subtly excluded as they exchanged quick smiles or laughed at private jokes.

Harriet couldn't understand it. Lewis hadn't appeared to be tiring of her. Their last session together had been the best ever, and yet now it looked as though it was all over.

Later, Lewis left the house and then Chris joined the two women. He barely spoke to Harriet, managing a brief greeting but refusing to meet her eye. With Rowena though he was so intimate that once again Harriet felt like an interloper. He touched her as intimately as Lewis had touched her, and once he bent his head and kissed the top of her spine where the vertebrae were exposed by the scoop neck of the blouse she was wearing. The sight of the kiss on the tender flesh sent a shiver through Harriet. She didn't want Chris, but she longed for Lewis to kiss her in the same way.

Confused and frustrated she passed the day as best

she could on her own, swimming in the pool, using the sunbed and later walking in the garden. By this time Lewis had returned. He stood next to his wife and together they watched the tall, slim figure wandering along the path at the side of the house.

'She's missing you already,' said Rowena.

'Good; that means she'll miss me even more by the end of the week. You and Chris have kept Friday night free?' His wife nodded, and her belly stirred at the prospect of what lay ahead for them all.

That night, despite what had happened in the day, Harriet still lay awake hoping that Lewis would come to her, but he didn't. She waited until two in the morning and then slept fitfully, her body – so well tutored in recent days – reluctant to rest without the sensual pleasures it was used to.

The next night Harriet used her hands to pleasure herself but although she gained physical release it wasn't the same and afterwards she cried into her pillow. She'd tried to pretend her hands belonged to Lewis, had conjured up an image of him as her fingers teased her clitoris, but it hadn't worked. The price of satisfaction was too high and she vowed not to attempt it again.

With every night that passed, Harriet became more

and more short-tempered. Rowena, aware of what the younger woman was going through, pretended not to notice and was kindness itself. Lewis kept out of Harriet's way, even taking his meals in his study under the pretext of work.

By the Friday night Harriet didn't know what to do. It seemed that Chris had been right in saying that Lewis never stayed constant to any woman for more than a short period, yet she was still certain that their intimacy had been more than physical. She longed for the courage to speak to him, to ask what had gone wrong, but on the few occasions that she'd had the chance her nerve always deserted her.

When she retired to bed she had a shower, then put her night light on and began to read a novel. Even the feel of the satin sheets against her skin worked as a reminder of her thwarted sensuality. Wriggling between them she recalled the way Lewis had dried her in a towel and then covered her in massage oil, and her toes curled at the memory.

When a light tap came at her door she decided she must have misheard. She'd ceased to expect Lewis any more. The tap was repeated, and this time the sound was unmistakable. 'Who is it?' she asked nervously.

'Who do you think!'

At the familiar sound of Lewis's voice Harriet was out of bed and opening the door in seconds, shamed by her own eagerness but unable to control it. She did at least manage to look surprised as she let him in. 'What do you want, stranger?' she queried lightly.

Lewis smiled down at her. 'I haven't come to read you a bedtime story!'

'I'm reading to myself,' she said, gesturing towards the open book on the bed.

'Can't you think of anything you'd rather do?'

She wished she had the strength of character to send him away, to say that he couldn't play these games with her, ignoring her for days at a time and then turning up as though nothing had happened, but her body needed him so badly that she rejected the thought at once. Besides, if she was to gain any kind of place in his affections then she knew instinctively that whining and complaining wouldn't do it.

'May I finish my chapter first?' she asked sweetly.

If it hadn't been for the rapid movements of the swell of her breasts, clearly visible above the lace of her nightdress, Lewis would have been inclined to believe her casual tone. As it was he admired her attitude, and felt a rush of affection for her. 'As long as you take off your nightdress, sit cross-legged on the bed as you read and I'm allowed to watch you,' he retorted.

'You can watch,' conceded Harriet, 'but until I've finished you can't touch.'

Realising she was serious Lewis had to sit at the foot of her bed and for the next five minutes endured the kind of physical frustration he'd forced on her for a week. He found that he didn't like it at all. Finally Harriet closed the book and smiled sweetly at him. 'I do like a good mystery! Now then, tell me what you had in mind.'

'I want you to put these on,' said Lewis, placing a cardboard box on Harriet's bed. She opened it, pushed aside the layers of tissue paper and drew out a white suspender belt, white stockings and a flimsy white camisole top with holes for her nipples. 'I like to see women partially clothed at first,' he said by way of explanation. 'It's much sexier, don't you think?'

Harriet was beyond thinking at all. She wanted his hands on her as soon as possible, but she knew that he liked to extend lovemaking, that it was always pro-longed and varied with him. Although she'd never worn a suspender belt before she found once the outfit was on and she'd paraded in front of her bedroom mirror that he was right, it did look extremely erotic.

Lewis stripped off all his clothes and then brought in the wooden chair from Harriet's bathroom. He placed it in the middle of the floor and sat down on the padded seat, his erection already pointing upwards. 'Come and sit on my lap,' he murmured. 'Face the mirror and lean back against me, that way we can watch ourselves at the same time.'

Obediently Harriet lowered herself across his thighs and she felt the silk stockings rubbing against his bare flesh. One of his hands glided over the the area of skin between her stocking top and hip bone while the other went round her upper body and spread itself over her left breast.

'Look in the mirror,' he urged her.

Harriet looked, and was startled by the expression of sensual abandon in her eyes as she pressed her back against his chest and spread her legs wide over him. Her naked vulva was damp with desire and when he began to massage her breast she started to tremble from head to toe at the blissful familiarity of his movements.

Her body, starved of attention for too long, leapt into life and Lewis knew that it was going to be difficult to do what he had to do unless he was very careful. Already Harriet was squirming against his legs and the flush of arousal stained her neck and chest. 'Keep still,' he whispered. 'We've plenty of time.'

Harriet didn't want to play the delaying game this time. Her body felt ready to burst with suppressed need and she had no intention of doing as Lewis said. She allowed the excitement to build and the exhilarating pre-orgasmic tingles darted through her vulva and lower belly so that she gave a groan of gratitude.

Lewis slid his right hand between her thighs and brushed his fingers over the tips of her curly pubic hair, allowing her only the faintest pressure. Harriet jerked upwards, desperate for greater stimulation but he moved his hand away again and the tendrils of desire that had begun to throb behind her pubic bone flickered briefly and then started to fade.

'Lewis, hurry up!' she begged him.

'Look at yourself,' he urged her. 'Have you ever seen anything so wanton?'

Glancing in the mirror she saw that she looked totally different. Her cheeks were flushed, her eyes huge and she was wriggling and rubbing against Lewis in a way that would have been unimaginable in her days with James, but she didn't care. This was what she liked, what her body adored and this man was the one she knew she had to keep with her for ever.

'Touch yourself,' said Lewis, moving his right hand upwards in order to stimulate her breasts but leaving her lower body alone. Frantically Harriet obeyed, knowing that if her clitoris didn't soon receive the stimulation it was screaming for, she'd go mad. Her fingers slid down the channel between her outer lips until they located the hard little button and as soon as contact was made her legs began to stiffen.

Lewis felt her body tense and he kissed the side of her neck while his hands massaged her breasts through the camisole in a soft kneading motion, sometimes drifting down the sides and beneath her armpits to tantalise the highly sensitive flesh there.

Harriet was moaning now, but she wanted it to be Lewis who triggered her climax and so as her outer lips opened wide and wetness flooded her tissue she reached upwards for one of his hands.

He knew that she was right on the edge, that she needed only one more delicate brushing movement across the clitoris, one rotation of his hand on her lower belly and she would be there but this was the very thing she couldn't have, not if the plan was to work.

To Harriet's astonishment he caught her hand and held it tight, then his left hand grabbed her left wrist and he stood up so unexpectedly that she would have fallen forward if he hadn't kept a tight hold on her wrists.

Shocked she stared at them both in the mirror. He tall and suddenly stern-looking, she struggling against what was happening while her aroused flesh screamed for relief.

'What are you doing?' she asked in bewilderment. 'I was about to come!'

He smiled at her in the mirror. 'Wouldn't you like to share your pleasure?'

'Share it?' she asked stupidly.

'Why don't we let Rowena and Chris watch?' he suggested softly, his lips warm against the nape of her neck.

Harriet tried to wrench herself free. 'No!' she protested vehemently. 'I just want you.'

He sighed. 'Then we'll have to take a break and start again a little later.

'Why?'

'Because I'd been looking forward to letting them see

us together. If we're not going to, I might have some trouble satisfying you just yet.'

Harriet was bewildered. She could tell how excited he was by the rock hard erection nudging against her. That was proof enough of his desire – he couldn't possibly need a rest.

'Don't do this, Lewis,' she begged him, attempting to turn and press her aching flesh against his naked body. 'Please, I need you now.'

He let his mouth continue kissing the top of her spine but at the same time drew her hands behind her back and then imprisoned her wrists in one of his large hands. The movement meant that her breasts, so swollen and hard from his touch, were jutted forward yet more proudly and she could see her nipples standing out through the holes in the camisole.

'Let's join them,' he whispered again as she shivered beneath the teasing lightness of his mouth aginst her vertebrae. 'Think how Rowena will envy you. Besides, it will be a new experience for you. I thought you wanted new experiences.'

Harriet tried to think straight, but it was difficult when her body was throbbing and tight with its own needs, and after being deprived of Lewis for several days all she could think about was the totally consuming pleasure he would bring her.

'I don't know,' she said hesitantly.

In the mirror she saw him lift his head and frown. 'You could have stayed safely with your fiancé, or secure in your old job if you hadn't wanted to expand your horizons,' he pointed out. Then he dropped his voice. 'I want them to see us,' he said persuasively. 'Rowena will be stunned when she sees us together.'

It was this which convinced Harriet, together with the incessant urging of her body. She wanted Rowena to witness her and Lewis making love. The prospect of his wife being forced to witness the way their bodies responded to each other was unbearably exciting and to Lewis's relief she finally nodded. 'Yes,' she said softly. 'I want them to see us too.'

She expected him to suggest they changed rooms but instead he simply went to the door and opened it. Rowena and Chris walked in. At that moment Harriet realised that the idea hadn't been a sudden one, but a carefully plotted plan and that he had always known she would accede to his wishes.

Rowena smiled at the younger woman. She was wearing a short shocking pink A-line skirt with a fitted black and pink short-sleeved top and her legs were encased in black stockings with a long seam down the back which, coupled with her black stiletto shoes, made a very sexy combination.

Chris looked as though he'd come from working out in a gym. His casual long-sleeved cotton top and track-suit bottom seemed incongruous next to Lewis's nakedness, but almost as soon as he was in the room he stripped them off to reveal his naked chest, covered in tight fair curls, and beneath his trousers he was wearing a pair of tight-fitting black briefs.

'You look very attractive, Harriet,' said Rowena huskily. Lewis's hands tightened round Harriet so that his wife could examine her at her leisure. Harriet tensed against him. This wasn't what she'd expected. She'd thought that Rowena and Chris would simply watch, not touch her themselves.

The film star ran her hands up beneath the flimsy camisole, drawing a delicate line along each of the ribs in turn. Then she withdrew her hands and looked at the nipples now sticking out through the holes in the top. With a soft laugh she moved her head and her tongue flicked at each of them in turn, sending tiny vibrations through the other woman's breasts.

Dark Secret

Helpless, Harriet squirmed and despite her shock she felt her arousal growing again. Rowena ran a finger beneath the top of the suspender belt and the stomach muscles contracted beneath her touch. Lifting the lower lacey edge she let her tongue dip into the quaking belly button and at this Harriet's body jerked, pushing her hips forward.

Rowena's eyes were bright. 'She's certainly very responsive,' she murmured, turning to her half-brother.

Chris, who'd been standing at a distance watching, moved to Rowena's side and they kissed each other lightly on the lips before looking back at Harriet. 'I knew she would be,' said Chris. 'I think we're all in for a very exciting night.'

Chapter Eight

'*SHALL WE LET* her have an orgasm before we begin in earnest?' asked Lewis, his arms wrapped round Harriet's upper body, pinning her arms to her sides.

Rowena looked thoughtfully at the girl. 'I think so. It should make what follows easier.'

'If I keep hold of her then you can use your skills,' said Lewis.

'I want you to do it,' protested Harriet, determined not to keep silent despite the unexpected turn of events.

'I'm afraid that tonight what you want isn't our paramount consideration,' said Rowena. 'Lewis has kept you more than satisfied in that direction. Tonight we want to see just how far you can be taken.'

'Why?' asked Harriet, shocked at the casual amusement in her employer's voice.

'Because it will be fun. Besides, Lewis seems to think you're something special. Chris and I want to see if it's true.'

Lewis's grip tightened for a moment and he made soothing sounds to comfort Harriet but some of her fear was already dissipating. If this was a challenge, if Rowena wanted to see whether Harriet was capable of holding a man like Lewis for any length of time, then she would show her that she could.

With her upper body unable to move Harriet stared at herself in the mirror. Her nipples were still peeping through the holes in the silk camisole top and she realised that if anything her excitement was increasing with every passing second.

'Spread your legs further apart,' said Rowena. Harriet did, and watched as Rowena opened a large handbag and drew out an electric toothbrush. She glanced up at the other woman for a moment, then withdrew a tube of gel. Carefully she parted Harriet's outer sex-lips and then spread some of it over the delicate tissue.

The gel was cold and Harriet gave a tiny gasp of

surprise. At once Chris stepped forward and in his hand was a tiny riding crop. He flicked it over the flesh beneath the suspender belt and immediately a thin red line appeared. Harriet screamed.

'You're meant to keep silent while Rowena works,' said Chris shortly. 'Every time you make a sound you'll feel the crop.'

The burning sensation of the blow was changing now, and thrills of arousal followed. Rowena, working between Harriet's thighs, turned to her brother. 'She liked that, she's become far more moist. Do it again.'

'No!' protested Harriet, and at once the crop fell, this time at the base of her camisole top.

'Keep silent,' Lewis urged her.

Rowena watched as Harriet's juices started to flow more copiously and she mixed those with the gel so that soon the entire area was throughly wet. Now she picked up the toothbrush and put it on the lowest setting before letting it travel up the straining girl's inner thighs.

Harriet heard her breath quickening and tried to subdue the sound. She didn't want the crop, despite the strange burning thrill of excitement that followed each blow. The brush head was small and delicate, the touch insidiously arousing, and Harriet longed for it to touch her where the gel had been spread but Rowena refused to hurry.

She moved it into the join at the top of the inner thighs and across the skin above the line of her pubic hair but it was lower down that Harriet's body was straining for contact and despite herself she gave a low groan of need.

When the crop flicked across her nipples she slammed back into Lewis with shock. His tongue flicked into her ear, sliding round and then jabbing into the earhole in simulated intercourse. Her nipples felt on fire, but they were throbbing, the blood coursing through them as her whole body screamed for satisfaction.

'You're so near, aren't you?' whispered Rowena against Harriet's belly. Harriet nearly answered her, but was stopped by a warning squeeze from Lewis. The film star laughed. 'Well done! I think perhaps it's time now. Are you tingling here?' and her finger circled the hard nub of the clitoris.

This touch alone started the strange darting feelings that Harriet so enjoyed. They moved within her pelvis and belly as her muscles gathered themselves together and her nerve endings responded to the urgently needed touch.

'I'm sure you are,' continued Rowena, and finally she held the outer lips apart with her left hand and moved the toothbrush to the screaming tissue so wickedly tantalised already.

At first the brush was held against the opening of Harriet's vagina and then with tortuous slowness it moved in tiny circles upwards until she felt the tingles inceasing and electric sparks shot through her, while her breasts burgeoned.

Rowena watched the clitoris closely. As Harriet's excitement began to peak it started to withdraw beneath its protective hood and she quickly pulled upwards on the skin above it so that it had nowhere to hide before allowing the bristles to caress the most sensitive part of Harriet's body.

The touch of the rotating softness against her screaming nerve endings at last triggered the climax Harriet had been waiting for. Suddenly the sparks lanced right through her, her thighs tried to close and then she was lost in the throes of release as everything came together and her body doubled forward with the uncontrollable contractions of her muscles.

'There,' said Rowena to her husband. 'That should have warmed her up nicely.'

As Harriet's body calmed and her breathing returned to normal she felt a terrible sense of shame and averted her eyes from Rowena and Chris. 'Now for a change of location,' said Lewis, quietly, and she found herself being picked up in his arms and carried along the second-floor landing to his bedroom.

Unknown to Harriet this had been carefully prepared beforehand, including the installation of concealed video cameras. Lewis knew that during the ensuing excitement he wouldn't be able to remain detached, and had decided to record the entire scene so that he could play it back later and watch their various expressions and attitudes the next day. That way he hoped that he would be able to see the truth for himself, and the ending of his film might finally become clear.

The curtains had been drawn and the main light extinguished, only small wall lights were on but above the bed several bright spotlights were carefully angled around the entire room.

'Can I change her clothes?' asked Chris, his voice shaking at the prospect.

Lewis nodded and placed Harriet in the centre of his

large bed. She lay looking up at him in dazzed incomprehension. He seemed to be as happy to share her as he had been to share his wife, and the realisation chastened her. She'd been so sure that she was different, that his feelings were special, that she'd never considered the possible dangers of their affair. Only now, when she was entirely at the mercy of the three of them, did she fully understand the risk she'd taken. And now was too late.

The next thing she knew, Chris's hands were unfastening her white silk stockings, peeling them slowly down her legs while his fingers stroked the smooth flesh of her legs. Then he unfastened her suspender belt, removed it and finally eased the straps of her camisole top down her arms before rolling it down across her breasts, making sure that his fingers flicked at the still aching nipples as the material was drawn away.

Naked and vulnerable she waited, her body taut and trembling with a mixture of fear and desire as the three of them studied her nude figure. 'She'll look good in the playsuit,' said Rowena.

'Excellent idea,' replied Chris. Quickly he manhandled her to the edge of the bed and then she was being squeezed into a plunging cupless black leather playsuit.

It zipped up the centre, ending between the undersides of her breasts. There was a black collar with a ring at the back, and a second zip to allow easy access between her thighs, but for the moment this was closed and she felt the pressure of the leather against her vulva.

Now her hands were drawn behind her back and fastened with soft padded handcuffs and then she was pushed in front of a mirror to look at herself. The sight of her firm creamy breasts hanging free beneath the leather collar, slightly lifted by the underwired edges of the corset part of the suit astounded her. She looked even more wanton than she had during sex with Lewis and without thinking she thrust her shoulders back further to emphasise her sexuality.

Chris laughed. 'An exhibitionist! Wonderful! I'm afraid you'll have to wait a little though. It's your turn to watch now.' He drew a fine chain through the ring at the back of her collar and fastened her to one of the bedposts. Here she was visible to one of the cameras and also free to see what was happening in the room.

Rowena watched the transformation of Harriet from cool efficient PA to a tousle haired leather-clad temptress with fascination. She wondered how well she would perform. The clothes were only the start for

Chris's games of domination. A thrill ran through her as her half-brother spoke. 'Hands behind your back, Rowena. Lewis has a present for you, haven't you Lew?'

His brother-in-law nodded, and then bound his wife's hands tightly with leather cord before covering her eyes with a black silk scarf and knotting it securely at the back of her head. 'Kneel on the carpet, Rowena,' he said quietly. Rowena remained standing. Resistance always increased her pleasure, but normally Lewis wouldn't play the game the way she liked it – he never seemed to relish the power it gave him over her.

This time it was different. His hands grabbed her fiercely at the back of her neck and then he was pushing her down, forcing her on to her knees in seconds. Then he released her and she strained to hear where he was, but it was difficult as the scarf covered her ears as well.

Harriet watched and found that her mouth was dry. Her breasts began to ache and she could feel the pressure of the corset beneath them. Chris, who was watching her, casually fondled each breast in turn and she heard herself sigh voluptuously at his touch.

Lewis, who was walking round to the front of

Rowena, glanced across and his eyes widened in surprise. He'd expected Harriet to be more cowed, at least initially, but she already seemed to be revelling in what was happening.

Reaching down, Lewis caught hold of Rowena's head and guided her mouth towards his straining erection. She parted her lips and teased the sensitive tip with her tongue, tasting the salty tang of him as she worked. She loved it when she was blindfolded – every other sense was so heightened that it doubled her pleasure.

Lewis's hands dug into her hair and he began to move his hips, thrusting in and out of her mouth far faster than he usually did. She struggled to accommodate him. Then, when he felt himself nearing orgasm, Lewis stopped her with his hands and withdrew.

Rowena felt bereft. She'd wanted Harriet to see Lewis ejaculate into her mouth, but Lewis had spoiled it for her and she experienced a moment's rage. His hand descended on the back of her head again and he kept pressing until her forehead was resting on the carpet. It was an awkward position and totally exposed her buttocks to the gaze of those standing behind her, including Harriet.

Now Lewis went over to Harriet. He drew a long ostrich plume from beneath his duvet and started stroking her breasts with it in such slow, teasing movements that she had a desperate desire for a hard touch, even the flick of the crop, anything to distract her from the relentless soft teasing of the plume that made her breasts ache and started the familiar throbbing beneath the zip fastener between her thighs.

In the meantime Chris had taken up his position behind Rowena. In his right hand he held the riding crop and using alternate backhand and forehand strokes he began to strike her on each of her buttocks in turn. Every blow was light but the stinging sensation it engendered was strong and Rowena couldn't help moving her buttocks in an attempt to evade the blows. Chris was too clever for her and anticipated every move so that soon the cheeks of her bottom were glowing a soft pink and her vulva began to open, the sex-lips flattening outwards in readiness for the penetration she longed for.

Harriet, still being stimulated by the unbearable delicacy of the plume, watched and her stomach, so tightly encased in leather, felt it would burst. She shivered at the touch of the leather beneath her and moved her hips to try and stimulate herself more. 'Keep still, Harriet,' said Lewis sharply, but his eyes were dark with longing for her.

Rowena was making strange mewing sounds now, her upper body swaying from side to side as she brushed the tips of her breasts over the soft pile of the carpet. Chris smiled to himself and with one final crisp flick of the wrist stepped away from her.

Now he and Lewis changed places again, and at last the incessant soft brushing on Harriet's breasts stopped and she let her head fall back against the bed-post in relief.

Lewis covered a double-headed vibrator in the gel that Rowena had used on Harriet earlier in the week and then let the heads rest against her two openings. Rowena felt the slippery hardness of them and thrust backwards towards him, straining for something to fill her aching flesh but Lewis simply tapped them softly against the rim of her rectum and the front of her vagina, and suddenly she felt the warmth of the gel as it came into contact with her skin.

Realising that once the two prongs were inside her all her delicate inner tissue would be subjected to the burning heat she froze, unable to believe that Lewis would be willing to push her to such extremes of sensation, but when his free hand pressed against her spine she knew from the size of the fingers that it was indeed him and not her half-brother.

Lewis teased her a little longer, knowing that anticipation would increase her fear of the gel, and then he slid the twin dildo in with a smooth twisting action, making certain that the sides touched the flesh of the walls of both her passages and within seconds her lower body was twitching and jerking. Ignoring this he slid the dildo back and forth, forcing yet more nerve paths to be aroused until Rowena felt she would go mad with the burning itching sensation that set her flesh leaping, while at the same time the rhythmic movements of the two prongs brought her closer and closer to orgasm.

She knew that when she climaxed the walls of both her rectum and vagina would close more tightly about the prongs and that then the glowing warmth would increase so she tried to stave off the moment. However, Lewis suddenly circled the vibrator so that her G-spot was stimulated, and when she cried out with pleasure he kept his hand motionless and concentrated on maintaining a steady pressure against the tiny place.

It was this that forced a wrenching climax from her and Harriet watched as the titian-haired star's body locked with tension and her head was thrown back while she screamed aloud as her muscles contracted and the gel was rubbed more firmly into her flesh.

With every contraction, every spasm, the warm flooding sensation increased until it seemed as though a fire was rushing up through Rowena's belly and even her breasts. No sooner had her first orgasm stopped than she was wracked by a second more intense one and when that was over she collapsed on to the carpet, sobbing with satisfaction.

Harriet knew that the leather between her legs was very damp. She could feel her juices flowing and her body longed to be part of what she'd seen. Chris crouched down and carefully unzipped her, releasing her vulva to the cool air. When he let an exploratory finger enter her, he drew some of the moisture from her vagina and spread it upwards along the highly sensitive stem of her clitoris.

'How does it feel?' he asked.

Harriet couldn't explain, couldn't begin to tell him about the pulsating heat that was consuming her.

'I want to know,' he insisted.

'I'm so hot,' moaned Harriet, her body perspiring beneath its casing of leather.

Chris was prepared for this. He reached for the ice bucket that was at his feet and then very carefully slid one inside the opening between Harriet's thighs. At the feel of the freezing cube against her flesh Harriet went still with shock, but he continued to ease it into her until it was just inside her and there it slowly melted, letting the cool water mingle with her body fluids.

Harriet shivered. The contrast was incredible, and then her eyes widened as he stood up and popped an ice-cube into her mouth. 'Suck on it slowly,' he instructed her. Harriet sucked, watched by Lewis who thought he might lose control and spill his seed on the carpet at the sight of her, she looked so magnificently wild and sensual.

Finally Chris drew an ice-cube over her breasts, rubbing it in circles round the nipples until she found herself leaning towards him, pulling against her chain in an effort to obtain contact.

'Can I take her now?' Chris asked Lewis.

Harriet stared at her lover, unwilling to believe he was going to allow this man to penetrate her, but almost excited at the thought. Lewis smiled at her. 'Yes,' he murmured. 'I want to see her come for you.'

The words almost made her climax, and her eager body strained harder. Chris released her from the bedpost and laid her on the bed, then re-fastened her hands but this time spread-eagled so that her body formed an X shape. The ice-cube inside her vagina had melted completely now and as Harriet watched, Chris readied his large penis. 'I want you to remember this,' he said softly, sliding a pillow beneath her hips. He spread some lubrication across the tip before sliding it into her, his hips moving in tiny circles as he penetrated a fraction at a time until at last he was deeply inside her.

'Use the quill pen on her clitoris,' suggested Lewis, fascinated by the scene. At once Rowena climbed on to the bed and as Chris increased the tempo of his movements Harriet felt the feather of the pen teasing her throbbing bud. Without any warning an orgasm tore through her, pushing her stomach upwards and wrenching at her abdominal muscles with the sudden shocking urgency of release.

Taken by surprise Chris could only watch the perspiration gathering on Harriet's skin and saw the rapid flush of arousal spread over her breasts and neck.

When she was still he withdrew, then slid back into her, his hands digging into the sides of her waist as he lifted her lower body the way he wanted it.

He was far rougher than Lewis, his movements less controlled, but Harriet's body was still aroused from the earlier stimulation and after a few minutes she felt another orgasm beginning.

'Wait for me,' said Chris, 'or you'll be punished.'

Harriet gasped and tried to quell her flesh, but then Rowena drew back the clitoral hood again and swirled the feather over the glistening nub, making self-control impossible. Harriet climaxed helplessly.

'I didn't mean to!' she protested as Chris stared down at her.

'That isn't the point,' he said coldly. 'You failed, which means that I have to punish you.'

Rowena saw the startled look on Harriet's face and smiled. 'Isn't Chris incredible? I adore his punishments.'

'I don't think I would,' moaned Harriet, struggling against her bonds.

Lewis watched the other three with interest. It was clear that Chris was fascinated by Harriet. She was the first woman he'd responded to apart from Rowena, and Lewis wondered how Rowena felt about that.

From the expression on her face he guessed that she wasn't pleased. He wished that he could see inside her head, discover how much of her jealousy was over him and how much over Chris. For a time he'd thought that the experiment was driving her towards him, and Chris was being excluded. Now he wasn't sure.

Strangely he didn't mind as much as he'd expected. He realised that he was actually more interested in Harriet, and Harriet's response to the night's adventures. In his original idea, the catalyst – at that time faceless and characterless – had been of no importance as a person. Her purpose had simply been to force Rowena into making a choice. It was different now. Harriet was flesh and blood, and very much a person in her own right. A person whose responses were beginning to be of more importance to Lewis than Rowena's, and that meant that the film wasn't going to work in the way he'd intended.

He couldn't do anything about it though. He had to accept what happened or the experiment was pointless. One possible problem of the new development was that there might need to be a change of emphasis in the casting. The heroine might not be Rowena, but Harriet. This thought did trouble him, because Rowena would never accept it. He gave a small sigh, wondering if this time his project had been too ambitious.

'Let me up,' said Harriet, having discovered that it was impossible for her to get free without help from one of the others. 'I don't want to be tied down any more.'

'Don't you understand that the choice isn't yours?' asked Rowena, running a hand caressingly round the exposed breasts and enjoying the instant response of the nipples.

'Lewis!' called Harriet beseechingly.

Drawn out of his reverie he looked over to the bed. He was already hard with desire and the sight of Rowena playing carelessly with Harriet's body while the younger woman attempted to subdue her clearly visible response aroused him even more.

'What?' he asked huskily.

'Please untie me,' she begged him.

'Let her go,' said Lewis curtly.

'She's to be punished!' protested Chris.

'I know that, but first let her sit up. We'll all have a short break. And take that suit off her, I want everyone naked.'

'I can undress myself,' protested Harriet as her hands

were freed, but she wasn't given the chance. As Rowena and Chris peeled the leather playsuit off her, their hands fondled and teased her at every opportunity until she was breathless from the sensations.

She went to get off the bed, but instead the other three joined her there, and they all sat cross-legged and naked while Rowena handed round a bowl of fruit. There were pears, soft ripe plums and slices of water melon. Harriet chose a golden pear with a delicate bloom of pink on it. When she bit into the fruit the juices ran down her chin, trickling on to her neck and breasts, but when she went to wipe it away Lewis stopped her. 'We'll clean each other up when we've finished!' he laughed.

Harriet watched Lewis bite into a slice of water melon. He leant foward to try and prevent it going down his chin and instead the watery juice splashed on to his upper thighs. He looked at Harriet, and it was as much as she could do to stop herself crawling across the bed and licking it off him there and then.

Rowena had chosen a pear as well and although she tipped her head back as she ate, the juice still spilt down over her chin and tiny fragments of soft pulpy flesh made their way slowly on to her abundant breasts.

It was Chris who broke first. He moved over to Harriet and started licking at the corners of her mouth, his tongue flicking delicately at the skin and then he nibbled his way down her neck, lapping at her from time to time like a kitten at a saucer of cream.

Lewis watched and felt his erection pulsating. For one brief moment he hated Chris. He'd wanted to do what his brother-in-law was doing, and the sight of Harriet closing her eyes and luxuriating in the touch of Chris's mouth and tongue inflamed him yet more.

Rowena glanced at her husband and was shocked by the rage in his eyes. She looked back at Chris and noticed that he was already erect again, and that he was no longer aware of anything but Harriet. A dreadful sense of loneliness gripped her. Bending her head she started to clean the water melon off Lewis's thighs.

As she worked her way inwards, letting her mouth nuzzle against the stem of his penis and inside the tender flesh of his inner thighs, Lewis wanted to catch hold of her hair and stop her. It was the wrong mouth. Despite the fact that this was what he'd wanted, that he'd intended to force Rowena to choose him over her brother, now that she was doing that he didn't want her. Realising that the story could not be allowed to resolve itself through his feelings, that it must be Rowena who decided, he made himself keep still and was about to respond by pushing Rowena on to her back and sucking the pear juice off her undeniably magnificent breasts when Harriet opened her eyes and looked at him.

For a few seconds she didn't seem certain who he was, she was so utterly lost in the sensuality of what Chris was doing to her, but then recognition dawned and she smiled at Lewis. It was an open, fearless smile; the smile of a woman confident in her sexuality and without thought he reached out a hand towards her.

Rowena caught his hand and guided it to her breasts. 'I'm still sticky, darling,' she said coolly.

'Then I must make you clean,' he laughed, but inside his stomach was churning. He knew that his feelings for Harriet were far deeper and more complex than for any women before her. The thought infuriated him, threatening as it did both his film and his peace of mind, and his response was immediate.

'In a minute Chris must decide on Harriet's punishment,' he said casually.

Harriet, who'd been watching him closely, was shocked. She'd felt sure she'd seen real affection in his eyes a moment earlier, but now his voice was cold and his gaze detached. As Chris lapped the last of the pear juice away he nuzzled her neck.

'I know just how to punish you,' he whispered. 'I shall use the brushes.'

Remembering the kind of games Chris and Rowena had played, Harriet didn't want any punishment from her employer's half-brother and she opened her mouth to protest, but Lewis covered it with his hand. 'Relax,' he whispered. 'Who knows, you might find you enjoy yourself.'

Before she'd had time to consider further, the other three quickly spread-eagled Harriet on the bed, and once more her wrists were fastened to the bed-posts, but this time her ankles were secured as well leaving her legs open and the area between her thighs totally unprotected.

'I think the blindfold again,' murmured Chris to Rowena, and once more Harriet was plunged into the world of darkness. She lay tensely, wondering what Chris intended to do to her, and whereabouts on her body he would start.

Lewis watched the fastened girl and his desire for her was so great that he could hardly breathe. The sight of her body, naked and totally in their power, was an even greater aphrodisiac than he'd expected, but he didn't want Chris to be the one to arouse new sensations in her. He wanted it to be him, and for the first time he disliked the role in which he'd cast himself for the duration of their experiment.

Rowena watched her husband and knew by the expression on his face that his feelings for Harriet were greater than any he'd ever had for her. No matter what happened as a result of tonight, he would never be hers in the way they'd both intended. Far from drawing them closer together, Harriet had succeeded in widening the gulf between them, and Rowena didn't like it.

She still wasn't sure which of the two men in the room she wanted to be with more, but she hadn't envisaged a situation where her choice might not be welcome. Lewis had always been the supplicant, trying to draw her away from Chris with a different kind of sexuality, a softer kind that after a time had bored her. He no longer looked like a man who would be interested. Rowena had never taken second place to another woman in her life, and the surge of jealousy that swept through her was astonishing in its power. She looked at her half-brother and felt a brief flicker of triumph. He understood her, and through him she could get her revenge.

'I'll help you,' she said softly. Chris smiled.

The hidden cameras rolled on, recording every flicker of emotion, every nuance of expression on all their faces for Lewis to view later.

For Harriet the wait seemed interminable. She could hear someone moving about, opening and shutting drawers and placing things on surfaces, and she heard Rowena's words but she still had no idea what was going to happen to her. Although tense her body had never felt more alive. Her skin was still sticky from the pear juice and her flesh seemed as ripe as the fruit itself, continually tingling with excitement even when no one was stimulating her. It was as though she was being taken over by her senses, and nothing mattered any more except sensation. Sensation and Lewis; the two were now indistinguishable in her mind.

All at once she felt Chris's arm brush against her shoulder and at once her body went taut with expectation. Her imagination had conjured up all kinds of strange things, but not once had she thought that what he would do was firmly but slowly pull a bristle hairbrush through her long locks. He was careful not to

pull or tangle her hair, concentrating instead on stimulating her scalp. The sensation was both soothing and
invigorating as the movement of the brush lulled her
while the touch of the bristles on her scalp made the
nerve endings there tingle.

She let herself relax into the sensation and her whole
body became soft and pliant. Lewis watched the way
her upper thighs fell further apart and her breathing
became deeper.

Once Chris's rhythm was established and Harriet
successfully lulled into a state of languid acceptance,
Rowena took a tiny baby's hairbrush in her hand and
carefully brushed it down the insides of Harriet's
imprisoned arms. The caress was like a whisper, so soft
as to render Harriet uncertain it was even happening at
first, but then as it continued her flesh responded.

The skin there was tender and receptive. Sometimes
Rowena used the brush in circles, sometimes in straight
lines, but she worked ceaselessly on the same area until
at last the pleasure became more of an irritation and
Harriet wanted the soft caress to move to other parts of
her body.

Rowena knew that this happened; Chris had done it
to her often enough so it gave her immense pleasure to

watch Harriet's mouth tighten in a grimace as the brushing continued.

Lewis saw Harriet's hips start to move and she twisted her upper torso as much as her bonds would permit to try and force the brush into contact with another area of skin. Only when she gave a tiny moan did Rowena move, and then she let the brush drift across the centre of the upthrust breasts until both the nipples were red and swollen. Once her object was achieved she changed the brush for a fine-pointed artist's paintbrush and after licking it swirled it around the rock hard buds making Harriet's whole body quiver with rising desire.

All the time his half-sister was working, Chris was continuing to brush carefully at Harriet's hair. Her whole scalp had now been massaged for over ten minutes and she didn't think she could stand it any longer. She tried to pull away from him, but escape was impossible and she heard him laugh to himself.

Her breasts were aching as Rowena continued to amuse herself with the engorged nipples, and when the brushing of her hair finally ceased Harriet didn't stop to wonder what would happen next, she was simply grateful for the respite.

Lewis studied Rowena and Chris. They were both totally absorbed in what they were doing, and worked like a well-established team on the hapless body squirming beneath them. He swallowed hard, trying to dampen down his ferocious need for Harriet that was causing him physical pain. He watched Chris's next move with interest, wondering how Harriet would respond.

Harriet, lying beneath the cruelly teasing touch of the slim, brush-point, couldn't make up her mind whether she was in heaven or hell. The sensations were exquisite, but although the result was a steady building of pressure within her, the touch of the brush alone wasn't enough to allow the build-up to progress beyond a certain point. As a result her whole body was tight and aching with need and there was nothing she could do to push her responses beyond the level Rowena and Chris permitted.

When Chris abruptly stroked the bristle brush across the tightly stretched skin of her abdomen, Harriet gave a startled cry and pressed herself down into the bed as she tried to evade him. Chris simply pressed the brush harder against the tender skin and smiled at Rowena as the younger woman shuddered.

The initial shockwaves startled Harriet, but then as blood coursed through the veins beneath her skin the sensation started to arouse a peculiar pleasure, different from any she'd known before. Thrills of dark excitement ran through her and when Rowena began to use the baby brush on Harriet's arm again while still continuing to tease her nipples with the finer brush Harriet's entire body started to scream for a climax, a release from the relentless build-up of tension.

Chris and Rowena were too experienced to let this happen. Time and time again Harriet felt her body gather itself together for the blissful explosion, and every time at the very last second one of the brushes would cease to move and the moment would be ruined until eventually Harriet was reduced to tears of frustration.

'Let me come, oh please let me come!' she begged them.

Chris bent his mouth to her ear. 'It's a punishment, remember?'

'I can't stand it any longer,' she moaned, but they both knew that she could. They changed rhythms and places, they brushed over her hip bones with the baby brush and up her calves with the bristle brush. They even allowed the finest brush to tease inside her inner lips, brushing briefly against her swollen clitoris so that her breath snagged in her throat and she wrenched her fastened body upwards trying to trigger the elusive orgasm. Again they were too clever for her – the brush had already been removed and her vulva moved restlessly against nothing.

Lewis continued to study them all. He had never seen a woman as swollen with desire as Harriet. Between her outspread legs he could see tiny beads of moisture, a clear indication of her arousal, and the whole of her upper body was flushed with sexual excitement while her breasts were larger and the veins in them more prominent than ever before.

He tried to imagine what such tension must be like, but it was impossible. All he could do was watch, and wait for the moment when he could take advantage of the cruel game Rowena and her half-brother were playing.

Harriet lost all track of time. It was as though the two of them had been toying with her for hours, and her body never seemed to understand the game. Despite constantly being let down, despite the continuing frustration and the terrible aching emptiness this caused, it responded to their every touch. She tried to stop it, to tell herself that there was no point and they weren't doing it to pleasure her, but still her skilfully trained body was misled by them as it searched frantically for the shattering moment of satisfaction their attentions promised.

Finally Lewis couldn't stand it any longer either. 'My turn I think,' he said quietly and the other two watched as he removed the final item from the table.

Chapter Nine

LEWIS CAREFULLY PULLED the soft latex ring over his penis until it was resting comfortably at the base. All around the ring were soft goose feathers designed to titillate the woman's clitoris as the man thrust. He knew from experience how well they worked, and the thought of the finely tuned Harriet at last receiving their soft caress on the most sensitive part of her body made him tremble. Slowly he approached the bed. 'Untie her,' he ordered Chris.

Chris frowned. 'She's meant to be kept like that.'

'Only for your pleasure. I prefer her loose.'

Rowena gave a small sigh. It was always the same; Lewis would never play games the way she liked them, not even now when so much was at stake. She nodded at her half-brother and he reluctantly released Harriet. 'What about the blindfold?'

'Leave that on for now,' replied Lewis, picturing the blissful shock that awaited Harriet when he finally penetrated her.

Harriet rubbed at her wrists, trying to restore the blood flow. Her flesh was screaming for attention, and the pressure in her body made it seems as though her skin had shrunk in the wash and was now too tight for the swollen flesh constrained within.

Lewis knelt over her, his legs outside hers, and looked down at her, savouring the moment. Her face was slightly flushed and damp with continual arousal, her hair tousled and her lips swollen and pink, but it was the desperate straining movements of her body that most clearly demonstrated her terrible need for sexual release.

More excited than ever before, Lewis bent his mouth to her ear. 'Bend your knees up towards your chin and rest your ankles on my shoulders, as close to my head as you can manage,' he told her.

At the sound of his voice, low and sensuous, she shivered and her legs moved up until she could feel the sides of his face with the insides of her feet.

Carefully Lewis balanced his weight on one arm. He then wrapped the other around her legs, just below her knees, so that he could control their movements and change the sensations for her once he'd entered.

Harriet's breathing quickened as she felt the soft velvet head of his erection nudging against her outer sex-lips and then he was gliding smoothly into her and at last the aching void was filled.

No sooner had she started to relish the feel of him deep within then she noticed another sensation as well. A light tickling feeling over her clitoris, like butterflies' wings brushing gently against it. When he withdrew a little the sensation stopped, but with every movement it started again, and sometimes he would rotate his hips so that the clitoris was stimulated even more and each time he did this Harriet heard herself gasping with pleasure.

At last the build-up towards release began again, but this time she knew that it wouldn't be stopped, that she would finally gain the satisfaction Chris and Rowena had refused her, and her body tried to rush towards its goal.

Lewis slowed the pace. His arm gripped her legs tightly so that she could feel him within her more, but her clitoris received less direct stimulation from the feathers. Then, as the darts of arousal from that tiny mass of nerve endings slowed he would release his grip a little and allow the feathers to touch her once more.

Without thinking Harriet reached up blindly for him and her hands went beneath his upper arms and gripped the back of his shoulders. He felt her fingers digging into him every time the feathers did their work and her body strained towards a climax, then when he withdrew the pressure of her fingers eased but she tried to pull him down towards her, seeking more physical intimacy from the position.

Toying with her like this, giving her such pleasure while at the same time increasing his own, was as wonderful for Lewis as it was for Harriet. Harriet though had been played with for too long, and soon she grew frantic and started to twist her lower body in order to increase the tempo of the pulse beating behind her aching nub.

Lewis decided to change position and delay her gratification just a little longer. Ignoring Harriet's pleas he disentangled their limbs and then knelt back on the bed with Harriet's hips positioned between his outspread thighs, before lifting her feet on to the front of his shoulders.

Her hands clutched at his knees and she moaned, pleading with him to end her torment. 'In a minute,' he whispered as his hands slid over her outer thighs and belly. Her muscles contracted violently at the touch and she pressed herself against him.

Lewis knelt up and the movement meant that he penetrated her very deeply while at the same time the feathers worked their usual magic against the sensitive tissue around her swollen clitoris. Before she could catch her breath he leant back and his erection pressed against the top wall of her vagina.

Harriet felt a deep ache start inside her, a blissful sweet ache that she didn't want to lose and she tried to move herself again. 'Keep quite still,' he said softly. 'Just wait.'

Harriet forced her writhing body to remain motionless, and Lewis kept still as well, concentrating simply on maintaining the pressure against her G-spot. He knew that if he kept the pressure constant for long enough she would almost certainly climax. Slowly her breathing quickened and her mouth opened slightly as the ache turned into something far greater.

Now it was ecstasy and it spread slowly upwards throughout her lower belly. When he saw her nipples tighten Lewis knew that her long-awaited orgasm was only moments away.

For Harriet the waiting, the stillness and the darkness caused by the blindfold were all part of the glorious sensation that was sweeping over her and then without warning the pulse behind her clitoris started beating frantically and her whole body drew in on itself as it prepared for the moment of release.

As she hesitated, balanced on the very edge of satisfaction, Lewis gently slid a hand beneath her buttocks and then pressed one fingertip against the rim of her anus. Again the pressure was firm and constant and combined with the pressure on her G-spot the result was incredible.

At last, after all the waiting, Harriet's body succumbed totally to the build-up of myriad sensations and the burning heat of her orgasm tore through her. Her arms and legs thrashed around wildly, her limbs totally uncoordinated in the final moment of sexual gratification.

Gradually the tremors of the orgasm slowed, and Harriet started to breathe more evenly, but then Lewis let his finger slip inside the rim of her anus and he ran it gently around the inside so that the dying embers of the climax were re-kindled and yet another violent wave of pulsating contractions tore through her. This time she let herself scream aloud, unable to control herself in any way, so totally was she in the grip of her body's sensuality.

As the second huge orgasm ripped through her, Harriet's vaginal walls contracted furiously and Lewis was no longer able to keep control. He held back for as long as possible, relishing the sensation of the pulsations that were gripping him, but finally his hips thrust furiously and then he was spilling himself into her, his climax going on and on until it seemed as though she would drain him of every drop of fluid.

When his last involuntary twitch had died away Lewis lowered himself on to Harriet, and she felt her breasts squash against his chest as he moved himself around, pressing against her as though trying for a closeness that was physically impossible. She clutched at him, trying to let him know that she wanted the closeness as much as he did.

Rowena and Chris watched the two of them and while Rowena felt jealous of Harriet, her half-brother was jealous of Lewis. He would have liked to see her writhe and scream for him in the way she had for his brother-in-law. His own erection was painfully hard now, and he was impatient for the night's games to continue.

'Isn't it time we all took part?' he asked casually, trying to conceal his eagerness from Rowena.

Lewis rolled off Harriet, lying by her side with one arm beneath her shoulders. He removed her blindfold and when their eyes met his softened in response to the look in hers. Harriet smiled. Lewis didn't; he would have liked to, but now was the wrong moment and he knew it.

Watching Harriet smile Rowena vowed to make sure the night ended as she'd planned. 'Come along, Lewis,' she said sweetly. 'You mustn't be greedy. Harriet's having such a lovely time you must let us all share her now.'

'We all share each other,' replied Lewis. 'Harriet's one of the group, not the focal point.'

'You could have fooled me,' murmured Rowena, averting her head as she spoke so that only Chris heard.

Harriet gazed at them all. 'I've never . . .' Her voice tailed off. It seemed ridiculous to start saying she'd never taken part in an orgy when she'd spent the past few hours being aroused and satisfied by three virtual strangers, but then she'd been passive. She wasn't sure she could take an active part when they were all involved.

Lewis looked thoughtfully at her. 'What's the matter, Harriet? Don't you find us attractive?'

'Yes, of course.'

'And haven't we given you a lot of pleasure?' asked Chris.

Harriet nodded.

'Then you must reciprocate,' said Rowena. 'Don't tell me you've still got some inhibitions left? Not after the past half hour!'

Harriet wanted to tell them that it wasn't a question of inhibitions, she knew she'd lost them long ago. It was a matter of feelings. She loved Lewis, she didn't love Rowena or Chris, and that meant that it was more difficult to lose herself in sensations. She responded more easily when her emotions were involved. Even when Chris and Rowena had been arousing her, she'd known that Lewis was watching, and hopefully being aroused by her. To make love to the others simply for their pleasure wouldn't be as easy.

'Don't disappoint me, Harriet,' murmured Lewis.

She smiled, knowing deep down that it wouldn't be too hard. Her sensuality was such that once her body was aroused again it shouldn't be difficult, it was only the prospect that was alarming. 'I'll try not to,' she promised.

'We don't have to stay in this one room, do we?' asked Chris. Lewis shook his head. 'Good, then let's go!' He grabbed Harriet by the hand and pulled her out through the door, along the landing and down the flight of stairs, stopping halfway down.

Rowena and Lewis were just behind them. All four of them were naked but the house was warm and Harriet realised that she was beginning to feel comfortable without her clothes, less self-conscious than ever before.

Chris stood with his back to the wall. 'Lie on your back on the stairs for me, Harriet,' he said. Rowena laughed. Puzzled, Harriet did as he asked. Chris then stood over her with his legs between her thighs and she drew one leg up so that her inner thigh was pressed against his outer leg. He raised his inner leg upwards, resting the knee on the same stair as Harriet's head.

Harriet saw at once what was intended as his erection bobbed just above her face. Reaching up a hand she slid it along his shaft, while at the same time Chris bent his outside leg. This had the effect of bringing his penis within reach of Harriet's mouth and also enabling him to stimulate her vulva with his shin bone.

Suddenly Harriet found herself tremendously excited by the whole experience. She could tell that Chris was desperate for her, that he wanted to come in her mouth and the sense of power this gave her was like an aphrodisiac.

She flicked her tongue along the underside of his shaft and sucked in her cheeks to create a vacuum within her mouth. The pressure on Chris's penis was intense and his legs trembled with the effort of keeping control for a few precious seconds as her velvet mouth and slightly tentative hands worked on him.

Lewis stood a few stairs above them leaning against the wall while Rowena rubbed herself against him, her arms round his neck and her perfect breasts brushing softly over his chest.

Although it was only a very short time since he'd climaxed with Harriet, Lewis found that the feel of Rowena against him together with the sight of Chris moving in and out of Harriet's mouth was making him hard again and he gripped Rowena by the hips so that she could feel his burgeoning erection.

All at once Chris gasped and far too soon for his liking he was spilling himself into Harriet's mouth. She sucked greedily at the liquid, enjoying the musky taste of him, and when he thought he'd finished she stroked a spot at the very base of his spine that forced a few last drops out of him. He groaned at the wrenching final contractions.

Rowena was determined to have some satisfaction herself now. Aware of this, Lewis continued down the stairs past Chris, who was leaning slumped against the wall, and the prone Harriet, and went into the large drawing-room. Rowena, who had followed him, went up on tiptoe to kiss him but he put her away from him and started throwing the large cushions from the chairs on to the floor.

By the time the other two joined them the floor was covered and with a laugh Chris threw himself down on to the soft surface. Lewis guided Rowena across and then the pair of them lay down facing her half-brother. Rowena leant back against her husband's chest and he supported himself on one elbow before sliding the other arm down the length of her side, lingering over her most sensitive areas until his hand closed about her upper thigh. He then pulled her leg back over his, tipping her on to her opposite side so that her sex was totally exposed to the watching Chris.

Harriet stood in the doorway watching. She saw Chris's hand move towards Rowena and then his fingers were carefully parting her outer sex-lips so that he could bend his head and use his tongue to part the inner lips.

Lewis glanced at Harriet. 'Come and join us,' he said with a smile. 'Sit by Rowena's head. I'm sure her breasts would like some attention.'

For just a second Harriet hesitated, but then, drawn by the excitement of the other three she moved to obey. She touched the redhead's firm right breast lightly and Rowena sighed. 'Not like that! Do it harder. I don't like soft caresses there.'

Harriet increased the pressure and at once Rowena's large nipples rose to twin peaks and Chris's tongue ran up and down the channel between her inner sex-lips in a soft movement that made her whimper with delight.

'Use your mouth on her,' Lewis suggested to Harriet. Bending her head she took one of the tight nipples between her lips and sucked on it. 'Nip it with your teeth,' continued Lewis. 'There's no point in wasting finesse on my wife, she doesn't appreciate it.'

His words excited Rowena and she rubbed herself against Chris's face. His tongue darted inside her for a moment, and then traced a quick path down her perenium before returning to the moisture-slicked inner channel.

Harriet waited for a few seconds and then she suddenly nibbled on the nipple imprisoned between her lips. Rowena gasped at the scarlet streak of ecstasy that shot through her and when she thrust her breasts further upwards Harriet bit her again.

At the same time Chris allowed his teeth to graze lightly against the stem of his half-sister's clitoris and at once she climaxed, shuddering violently for several seconds. Harriet released the other woman's nipples and watched her body shaking. She found it unbearably exciting, and suddenly wanted someone to pay her attention again.

Chris, lifting his head from between Rowena's thighs, knew from Harriet's expression how she was feeling and pulling her to her feet he drew her across the room to stand by one of the chairs. He bent her face down over the broad arm, her head hanging down in the space where the deep cushion had been, and before she had time to protest his hands were on her buttocks and he was separating the cheeks of her bottom.

Once she was fully open Rowena rubbed lubricating jelly all around the entrance to her rectum, occasionlly letting one small finger slip inside the rim, then she stood back and watched as Lewis, now fully erect again, positioned himself behind the girl.

Harriet held her breath. She knew what was going to happen, but not who was going to do it to her. When Rowena crouched at the front of the chair and began to massage Harriet's breasts she tried to turn her head to see which of the men it would be but Rowena caught her hair and kept her face down.

'It's a surprise,' she whispered. 'I expect you're hoping it's Chris. Lewis is so large, isn't he? Even I find it painful sometimes when it's Lewis. Not that I mind. I like the pain, but somehow I don't think you will.'

Lewis couldn't hear what his wife was saying, but he felt Harriet stiffen beneath his hands and knew that she was now tensed against him. Cursing beneath his breath he let one hand slide under her so that he could tease her clitoris, drumming lightly and insistently against the surrounding area until she grew slippery with excitement and her muscles relaxed.

Now he could let his swollen purple glans rest against that inviting puckered little opening and he circled his hips to encourage her to open more. Still the most secret of entrances remained closed against him. He stopped, uncertain whether or not to proceed, but then Rowena and Chris changed places and as Chris caressed the dangling breasts Rowena slid a well oiled finger into her husband's rectum, pushing until she could massage the prostate gland.

Immediately he was flooded with sharply intense sensations that nearly precipitated his climax and without thinking Lewis thrust blindly forward, his body intent on gaining its own satisfaction.

Despite the lubrication of the jelly and the stimulation that had preceded it, this violent intrusion made Harriet cry out with a mixture of pain and shock. He was so large he seemed to be stretching her more than her body could stand and she tried to twist away from him.

Lewis grabbed her hips to keep her still and slowed his pace a fraction and then Chris pressed his hand upwards against her belly. He pressed and released, pressed and released, then lowered his hand until it was just above her pubic bone. There he repeated the process and now sparks of delicious pressure filled her belly and when his fingers went lower and parted her pubic hair he kept the heel of his hand firmly in place so that her bladder was still under pressure.

Harriet felt she would burst. There was a hot sensation in her belly, her clitoris was throbbing and the almost painful movements within her rectum were now starting to engender delicious thrills that lanced right through her.

At that moment Lewis climaxed and his spasmodic jerking as he spilled his seed into Harriet for the second time in the evening triggered her climax and she felt her internal muscles contract gratefully while the delicious heavy fullness swelled and swelled until at last she came.

Eventually she stumbled from the arm of the chair and lay down on the cushioned floor with Lewis next to her while Chris and Rowena stared at each other, their eyes bright with a strange yearning excitement.

'What would you like us to do for you?' asked Chris.

Lewis looked at his wife with interest. All of them present, except for Harriet, knew that tonight was the film's final scene. It had been decided long ago that out of a night's prolonged sexual interplay would come the plot's resolution.

Nights like this changed people's feelings and perceptions. Sometimes they discarded old loves and ways for new ones; at other times they decided that they no longer wished to live as dangerously as before, choosing instead to be secure in a single relationship. Exactly what Rowena and Chris were thinking Lewis had no idea; all he knew was how he felt. As for Harriet, as the nameless girl in the film her feelings had never been considered important. Now he knew better. Harriet had changed the entire plot but he had to accept it. If he didn't then he could no longer tell himself that his films reflected life. However much he might have wished for something different, things were the way they were. Rowena had this one last chance to shape the finale.

'I think I'd like us all to use the sauna,' said Rowena. 'It's my favourite place.'

'I've never been in a sauna,' said Harriet innocently.

'All the more exciting for you then,' said Chris smoothly, already picturing how she would look as she emerged from the steam room and was shown what awaited her.

Lewis nodded. He was pleased now that he'd had the foresight to instal cameras in most of the main rooms. All that he'd missed of the night so far was the sex that had taken place on the stairs, and that vision was printed so clearly on his brain that it didn't need cameras.

Chris put an arm round Harriet's waist and squeezed her affectionately. 'You'll enjoy this,' he assured her.

Harriet didn't believe him. There was too much suppressed excitement in his voice, but she couldn't understand why because Ella used saunas regularly and was always trying to get Harriet to join her, claiming they put new life into her.

The four of them walked past the swimming pool and through some doors to the far end. In front of them was a large cubicle with darkened windows and Harriet hesitated.

'It's just steam,' Lewis told her. 'You might find it rather hot at first but you'll soon adjust. There are slatted shelves for us all to lie on.'

Rowena went in first and Harriet followed. The almost suffocating heat rose up and she coughed, but the men were on her heels and she was hustled into the cubicle before she could voice any misgivings.

The steam swirled about them and it was difficult to see where the shelves Lewis had mentioned were. Then she felt his arms on her hips and he guided her towards one of the lower ones, pressing her shoulders down so that she didn't hit her head on the one above.

Harriet lay back. Sweat trickled down the valley between her breasts then along her ribs. The entire surface of her body was covered in a film of perspiration and it was difficult to breathe.

'Don't you think it's bliss?' enquired Rowena from above her.

'Not really,' confessed Harriet. 'It's too hot.'

'You'll cool off quickly in the next room!' laughed Chris, and she felt his hand grip her ankle and caress her calf. Above her Rowena gave a small sigh of pleasure and Harriet realised that Lewis must be lying with his wife because she could hear the sound of flesh against flesh and the soft murmur of his voice.

When Chris's hands started to fondle her breasts she was sure that she was too drained by the heat to respond, but amazingly her nipples still sprung to life and encouraged by this he pressed his damp face between them, nuzzling at the inner surfaces.

'Time for the next room,' called Lewis.

Harriet was highly relieved, and let Chris lead her through the steam and out through a different door into the cubicle beyond. The cold hit her in an icy blast. Stunned by the change in temperature she backed away as goosebumps covered her skin and she began to shiver.

At the far side of the cubicle was a bath, but it wasn't full of water, it was piled high with snow. Harriet stared at it in astonishment, and then Rowena was climbing in covering herself with the icy flakes and laughing with pure joy.

'Aren't you going to join her, Harriet?' asked Lewis, his dark eyes unfathomable.

Harriet could feel her teeth chattering at the prospect. 'I don't think I can,' she protested.

'It's what they do in Finland,' he assured her. 'Believe it or not it's very invigorating once you take the plunge.'

Chris stood by the bath tub and waited. Rowena looked over at the shivering Harriet and smiled. If she hadn't done that, if she'd kept her feelings to herself, then Harriet might well have refused and left the three of them alone together but the sight of Rowena's pleasure at her discomfort spurred her on.

'All right,' she said briskly and then she was climbing into the freezing snow. For a moment she quite literally couldn't breathe as the biting cold snow covered her sweat-drained flesh.

Now the two men began to move the women around in the bath. Lewis worked on his wife, massaging the snow into her breast and belly, moving his hand between her thighs to press the freezing flakes against her sex mound and as he worked Rowena sighed voluptuously, relishing the shocking contrast after the jungle heat of the steam room.

Chris worked just as assiduously on Harriet. At first her body shrank from him, but then a wonderful glow started to suffuse her body and when he turned her on her face in the snow and rolled tiny snowballs up and down her spine every part of her began to tingle so that she felt more alive than ever before in her life.

'Our turn,' said Chris at last and the two women stepped out to let the men in. Now it was their turn to massage the snow into the men and when Harriet filled her hands with snow and then ran them up and down Chris's penis he gasped with excitement and reached up for her breasts, tweaking the rigid nipples and instigating blissful darts of excitement.

'How do you stop the snow from melting?' asked Harriet.

'The bath's really a kind of fridge,' explained Rowena. 'I paid a fortune for it, but it was well worth the money.' She looked at Harriet's body. 'You seem to appreciate it as well. I hope you like the final part as much!'

'I thought this was it,' said Harriet. 'Ella's never said there was anything more.'

'Well, whoever Ella is she doesn't know everything,' laughed Rowena.

Lewis and Chris climbed out of the tub and then shepherded the two women out of the cubicle and back round the side until they were at the side of the swimming pool.

'Lie face down on the loungers,' said Chris, producing two blindfolds. 'It's always ladies first on these occasions.'

The blindfolds were fastened and Harriet and Rowena stretched out on the slatted loungers, whose soft cushions had been removed. The slats pressed into Harriet's breasts, already tender from the sauna, but she didn't like to protest because Rowena seemed quite happy with her position.

The air around the swimming pool was pleasantly warm, and Harriet slowly started to relax after the contrasting heat and cold of the sauna. Her limbs felt heavy, and the darkness of the blindfold lulled her towards sleep.

She was drifting off, her thoughts full of Lewis and the night's events, when her body was stunned by a fierce stinging sensation across her buttocks. She jerked back into wakefulness and started to move from the chair. 'Keep still,' laughed Chris. 'This is the best part of all.'

Again she felt the piercing stinging sensation, but this time it was on her upper thighs and she closed her legs to protect herself. 'What are you doing?' she gasped, and even as she spoke she heard the sound of something falling against Rowena's skin too.

'It's only the birch twigs!' said Chris. 'They get your blood flowing again.'

He was clearly an expert at applying the bunch of sticks because each blow fell in a slightly different place until the whole of Harriet's back was smarting and pricking. She wriggled and at once the slats of the chair pressed into her lower belly.

'Now turn over,' said Chris, the excitement clear in his voice.

Part of Harriet didn't want to. She felt that she should refuse, tear off the blindfold and walk out of the room, but she could hear Rowena's tiny cries of rising excitement and knew that her own body was slowly responding in the same way.

At first the burning stripes had been uncomfortable, close to pain, but already that was changing and she was trembling with the beginnings of that dreadful need Lewis had kindled in her. She tried to imagine how the twigs would feel falling on her delicate breasts and belly and suddenly she wanted to know, to experience it for herself and so she turned and Chris looked down at her long, slim body and his legs went weak with desire.

Lewis paused for a moment, despite Rowena's pleas, and glanced at his brother-in-law. It was impossible for Chris to disguise the lust on his face and when he felt Lewis's eyes on him he turned to look at him defiantly.

'Enjoying yourself?' asked Lewis coolly.

'Very much,' retorted Chris, and Lewis watched the fair-haired young man raise his arm high in the air and bring the birch twigs down across Harriet's unprotected abdomen. She jerked with the impact, but her nipples were visibly hardening and as the tiny red marks appeared on her skin she thrust her belly up as though begging for more.

Chris was happy to oblige, and Lewis had to look away, angered both by Chris's excitement and Harriet's response. His blows on Rowena increased in force and she squealed with delight, lifting her buttocks high into the air to present an easier target for him.

Harriet was in an ecstasy of excitement. Her breasts were aching for what she now thought of as the caress of the birch twigs, but Chris continued to apply them to the lower part of her body until she grasped her breasts in her hand and pushed them up with a moan of need.

Seeing her like that, begging him to strike her in the way he liked best, Chris longed to take her there and then without consulting the others. He no longer cared about the rules of the plot, he simply wanted to take Harriet but first he allowed the twigs to strike her where she so clearly wanted them. The crispness of the blows across her breasts precipitated a sudden and unexpected orgasm in Harriet whose body shuddered and trembled before her arms and legs sprawled limply over the sides of the lounger.

At this Chris lost control. He hurled himself on top of her, moving roughly against the marked skin and nipping at the flesh of her throat and shoulders. Harriet, lost in the world of darkness and pleasure, was taken by surprise. She tried to push him off because this wasn't what she wanted, but Chris was beyond stopping. He reached under her and she felt his fingers moving urgently between her buttocks. Clenching herself against him she went to close her legs but found that he had a thigh between them and his erection was already nudging at the entrance to her vagina. He was heavy and rough, his hands careless of her needs as he struggled to achieve his own gratifaction.

'Stop it!' cried Harriet. 'I don't want you. Get off.'

Lewis, who hd been applying the birch twigs to Rowena's inner thighs, was suddenly alerted to what was happening. He dropped the switch and crossed over to where Harriet was struggling.

'What the hell do you think you're doing?' he asked Chris.

'She's enjoying it,' muttered Chris, still trying to force the cheeks of her bottom apart.

'Get off her,' Lewis's voice was filled with icy contempt. 'Can't you ever do what you're told?'

'She's not yours,' panted Chris, pressing down on Harriet's shoulders.

'She isn't yours either,' said Lewis coldly. 'Harriet belongs to herself. Now get off her.'

Rowena tore off her blindfold, sat up and looked over at her half-brother. 'What are you doing?' she cried in disbelief. 'That wasn't part of the script.'

Chris stared at his sister in a daze of sexual frustration. 'I want to do it my way. I want to hear her scream like you scream for me. I want . . .'

'You bloody fool,' said Lewis scornfully. 'She isn't like your half-sister. Any idiot could have worked that out for himself.'

'She is!' insisted Chris. 'She liked the twigs, she liked the pain, she . . .'

'Hurt *me*,' said Rowena softly. 'Come here, Chris. I want you to hurt me now. Please, I need you.'

Harriet lay quite still, more shocked by what she was hearing than by anything that had happened to her since she came to the house. They were talking as though this was some kind of play or film, not real life. And as for Chris, how he could have thought she wanted the kind of thing he and Rowena did she couldn't imagine.

Lewis watched his wife closely. She was holding out her arms to her half-brother and her need was there for them all to see. Very slowly Chris got up off Harriet and stumbled over to Rowena.

'You can do anything you like to me,' she whispered. 'Take me to your room. I want you to do everything you can think of. Take me further than we've ever gone before. I need you, Chris; she doesn't. She's no different from Lewis.'

'But if I had her, you could stay with Lewis!' protested Chris. 'We'd both be free then. Isn't that what you wanted?'

Rowena shook her head. 'What I thought I wanted and what I need are two different things.'

'But I want Harriet!' he protested.

Rowena stared at him. 'You can't do! Don't you understand, she isn't like us and she never will be.'

'I'd change. I'd be what she wanted. She excites me, Rowena. There's such sensuality in her response – she's so open to new experiences it makes everything more exciting. Like starting my sex life all over again.'

Rowena looked at her husband, her eyes bewildered. 'You can't both want Harriet!' she said in horror.

Lewis gave a twisted smile. 'Why not? I never promised you a happy ending.'

Chapter Ten

HARRIET STILL DIDN'T understand what was happening. She turned to Lewis. 'What do you mean, "happy ending"?'

Furious, Rowena decided to attack both men in the way that would hurt them most, by telling Harriet the truth. 'You don't really think my husband is in love with you, do you?' she sneered. 'He isn't in love with anyone. Lewis lives for his work, and you were just a part of it.'

'But I didn't do any work for him,' protested Harriet. 'Only a few letters and phone calls. It was you who employed me.'

'When I *employed* you it wasn't to write stupid

letters for either of us. You were chosen because Lewis thought you were attractive, and exactly right for the role of innocent pawn.'

None of this made any sense at all to Harriet, who hadn't understood a word Rowena said. 'Lewis wasn't there when you interviewed me,' she protested.

'He was watching through one of his two-way mirrors. I'm sure you know all about them, after all you did use one to watch me with Chris, didn't you?'

'How do you know that?' gasped Harriet.

Rowena laughed. 'Because it was all part of the plot, darling!'

'What plot? You aren't making any sense.'

'Lewis's film, the one I'm meant to star in, is about a brother and sister who are in love with each other. In the film the sister marries but the husband can't stop her continuing her affair with her brother. Both he and his wife want the relationship to end, only the woman is too caught up in the dark sensuality of her incestuous affair. Are you with me so far?'

Harriet nodded. It was beginning to make a horrible kind of sense.

'Good. Well, Lewis had the brilliant idea of bringing the film to life, and only writing the script as events happened. We had the perfect cast here, except for one vital ingredient – the other woman. He thought it needed an outsider, a catalyst, and that this young woman's presence would force all the characters to re-appraise their lives.

'Of course, in order for it to work the men had to become sexually involved with her, which Lewis did rather too convincingly I'm afraid, and then the heroine would decide which of the men she wanted the most. I was meant to choose between Chris and Lewis after watching them both with you. Do you understand now?'

Harriet stared at Lewis. 'So you never really felt anything for me? You were just playing out this charade in order to make your film truthful, is that it?'

'It's called *cinema vérité*,' said Chris helpfully.

'I call it a cheap, despicable trick,' said Harriet furiously. 'How dare you take someone into your home and then use them physically and emotionally for your work! Haven't you any conscience at all?'

'Not much,' admitted Lewis.

Harriet jumped to her feet. 'I hate you all. I think you're sick, and if this is what they call art I don't want anything to do with it. I hope the film's a flop and you never work again.'

Lewis reached out an arm and grabbed her by the wrist. 'Don't you see, Harriet, you changed everything. What Rowena says is true, but once you were here, once I got to know you, it didn't go the way I'd planned.'

'Really? How disappointing for you!'

'No, it wasn't. I didn't mind. Harriet, I do feel something for you. Sure the first time I took you to bed it was acting, but once we were together, once we'd made love, it changed. I tried to tell myself it hadn't, that I was just caught up in the role-playing, but deep down I knew even then. I don't want to lose you, Harriet. You mean more to me than any woman's ever meant.'

'According to your wife that isn't saying very much,' retorted Harriet. 'Tell me, does your work still come first?'

'No!' he protested, and Rowena drew in her breath in astonishment. 'Harriet, if you leave, I'll come after you. I can't let you go. When I saw Chris on top of you just now I could have killed him. As for watching you with him earlier, on the stairs, it was agony because I felt that you should be with me. I didn't want to go on with it all any more.'

'But you did, didn't you?' Harriet pointed out. 'You never stopped and told me the truth.'

'There was too much riding on it, I couldn't. But now it's finished, we can—'

'It's finished all right,' said Harriet, fighting back her tears. 'I'll never forgive you for what you've done to me. I want to leave now.'

'Wait!' interrupted Chris. 'Let me come with you. There's so much I could teach you. We'd be happy together once you admitted the truth about yourself. You know that you're fascinated by me, I can tell by your responses. Don't back away just when you're finding out who you really are.'

'None of you knows anything about truth,' retorted Harriet. 'You don't live in the real world, and you never will.' As she fled from the poolside the other three looked at each other in silence.

Up in her bedroom, Harriet started throwing clothes into suitcases, her heart pounding with shock and grief. She knew that nothing they'd told her had made any difference, that she was still as obsessed by Lewis as he claimed to be by her, but she didn't know how she could ever trust him again, even if he meant what he'd said about coming after her.

As for Chris, she shuddered at the thought of a life-time with him, although she also knew that there was a part of her, a part only just beginning to emerge, that did take pleasure from some of the things he did. But she didn't love him, and the knowledge that she did love Lewis made his betrayal all the more terrible.

In Rowena's bedroom husband and wife sat on either side of the bed. Lewis was staring moodily out of the window while Rowena sat with her head in her hands.

'How could it have gone so wrong?' she complained bitterly.

'It didn't go wrong,' said Lewis shortly. 'This is what happened. There never was a right or wrong ending.'

'But what about me?' she demanded. 'I'm meant to be the heroine. If you think I'm going to star in a film where I end up losing both men to some naive English girl with long legs you're making a big mistake.'

'You wouldn't be the star,' he said flatly. 'Whoever plays Harriet would be the star.'

Enraged, Rowena threw a book at him. It hit him on the back of the head and he turned on her, his eyes dangerously dark. 'You were the one who started this,' he said softly. 'If you remember, you begged me to make this film. "I want to be free of Chris" you wept, and I believed you. But it wasn't true, was it? You didn't want to be free of him at all, you wanted to humiliate me. All the way along it was Chris you were going to stay with. That was the ending you had in mind, but Chris has spoilt it by falling for Harriet himself.'

'I did want to be free of him!' protested Rowena.

'You're a rotten actress and a rotten liar. When I go through the films your face will give you away, but the few times I did see your expression I could tell that it was Chris you were most involved with.'

'What film?'

'You don't think I committed everything to memory tonight, do you? I filmed it all, and I intend to watch it carefully. Then I'll send for Mark and give him the ending.'

'What's going to happen to us all?' asked Rowena despairingly.

Lewis shrugged. 'Right at this moment I honestly don't care.'

'Do you really love Harriet?' asked Rowena incredulously.

Lewis sighed. 'I suppose I do. I certainly can't contemplate living without her.'

'But why? We had a good life together, didn't we?

And we're in the same business, we talk the same language. Harriet won't understand what you do. She'll be jealous of your work.'

'I was jealous of Chris – it didn't mean our marriage wasn't good for a time.'

'If you were jealous then you must have loved me!' exclaimed Rowena.

'No, it was my pride that was hurt. No man likes to think a woman prefers another man's style of lovemaking, especially when it's her half-brother.'

'She isn't even beautiful!'

'She's less obviously beautiful than you,' admitted Lewis. 'You're incredibly sexy-looking, but deep down, Rowena, I don't think you enjoy sex as much as you say. Not the kind of sex I enjoy anyway.'

'I only married you because you were handsome and famous,' said Rowena viciously. 'And you're right, your style of lovemaking never did suit me, but as long as I had Chris too I was all right. Now your bloody film's ruined everything. You say you can't live without Harriet – well I can't live without Chris. I don't care about acting, I don't think I ever want to make a film again, but I must have him. I need the charge he gives me, the excitement that you've never understood.'

'I understand it,' said Lewis. 'It just isn't my style. For a change, yes, but not all the time.'

'Then we'd be well rid of each other. Unfortunately Chris has decided he'd rather have Harriet, and Harriet doesn't want you.'

'Harriet did want me, until you decided to tell her the truth,' said Lewis angrily.

Rowena smiled sweetly. 'Don't tell me you'd have started your relationship based on a lie. That would be highly immoral!'

'Whatever happens you and I are finished,' said Lewis, getting to his feet.

'And who will you get to star in your film?'

'Believe me, once the script is completed I won't have any trouble with casting. It isn't as if you were a big draw any more. I was doing you a favour.'

Rowena scowled. 'As it turns out it was a favour I could have done without.'

'That's what's exciting about a venture of this kind. I have to admit, this isn't a twist I'd ever have thought up for myself.'

'Make sure you thank Harriet before she leaves then. I'm sure she'll appreciate having been such a help to you.'

Lewis slammed out of the room.

Harriet was closing her last case when she heard a tap on her door. Her heart missed a beat as she imagined Lewis standing on the other side. Despite all that had happened she knew that she wanted to see him one final time.

'Come in,' she called.

Chris entered. 'Are you really leaving?' he asked.

'Yes,' said Harriet curtly, almost in tears now that she knew it wasn't Lewis.

'I'd like to come and see you, after you've gone.'

'There's no point. I don't want to see you.'

He moved closer and his hands gripped her tightly round the shoulders. 'You know I can excite you. Earlier, beside the pool, you loved it when I used the birch twigs on you. That's only the beginning. Harriet. There's so much more I can teach you.'

'I'm sure there is, but I don't want to learn it.'

'Your body does. I can feel your nipples hardening at the thought,' he murmured, and his hands roamed over her breasts which were covered by the thin cotton material of her tie-blouse.

'All right, since you seem to need me to spell it out I will,' said Harriet. 'Perhaps you're right, maybe there

278

are things that you do that excite me, but I don't want *you* to do them.'

'You want Lewis, don't you?'

Harriet stayed silent.

'He won't ever let you explore your darker side. He wouldn't do it for Rowena, that's why she kept turning to me.'

'No it isn't!' shouted Harriet, furious with all of them, but most of all furious with her own body for letting her down at a moment like this. 'You and Rowena are tied together by far more than that. You're incapable of living apart. Even if I did love you, which I don't, you wouldn't stay faithful to me. You'd keep running back to your half-sister, because you aren't two people, you're two halves of one.

'I saw that for myself the first time I watched you together. Like it or not, Chris, you and Rowena are inseparable and no one but her will ever understand or appreciate you properly. Why won't you accept that?'

His light blue eyes stared at her. 'Perhaps because I'm afraid of what we'll do to each other,' he said at last.

'You both thrive on fear. You need that edge to everything you do. Think about it, Chris. Once you'd taught me all you know, where would we go from there? It's more than sex, you two are emotionally bonded for life. Your needs and desires are the same – no one will ever be able to satisfy either of you half as well.'

'You mean you aren't prepared to be as honest as she is about your sexuality,' he said contemptuously.

'No,' she said quietly, 'That isn't what I mean. I think I understand myself very well now, but if you want to think that's what I'm saying then fine, go ahead and think it. The bottom line is that you and Rowena are meant for each other, and there isn't any way out. You may not always be happy together, but you'd be far more miserable apart.'

Chris released her. He paused by the door. 'I thought you were special, but you're not. You're pathetically conventional, and you'd have bored me in a few weeks. I only hope Rowena will forgive me.'

'Don't worry,' said Harriet, turning her back on him. 'Rowena knows very well that she can't live without you. Now please get out of my room.'

'Just remember this, Harriet,' said Chris softly. 'You still haven't achieved your full sexual potential. If you do stay with Lewis, you'll have to encourage him to be more adventurous or you'll end up bored by him.' With that he closed the door softly behind him.

After he'd gone Harriet sank down on her dressing-table stool and stared at herself in the mirror. She didn't look very different from the day she'd come to the house for her interview, but inside she was a completely different person. If anyone had told her what she'd learn about herself during her time here she'd never have believed them.

Lewis hadn't only stolen her heart, he'd taken away her innocence as well but she was shocked to realise that she didn't care. She liked the person she'd become, liked the way her body responded to all stimulation and the new ecstatic pleasures she'd discovered. The trouble was, if she lost Lewis then where would she find another man who understood her body and its needs so well?

Unlike Chris, Lewis didn't knock on Harriet's door. Instead he walked straight into her bedroom, and found her gazing at herself in the mirror. She turned to look at him, her eyes expressionless. 'What do you want?'

'I've come to apologize.'

She raised her eyebrows. 'Isn't it rather late for that?'

'I never meant to fall in love with you, Harriet. It just happened. Then, when I admitted to myself how I felt it was too late. I couldn't tell you the truth or the film would have been ruined. I had to let events run their course. I was going to explain it all to you afterwards.'

'I don't suppose you'd have put it quite as bluntly as Rowena.'

'No. Because Rowena was angry she tried to hurt you. I never meant that to happen. You must have been able to tell that you were important to me.'

'I thought I was,' she said sadly.

Lewis walked up behind her and laid his hand on her shoulder, staring into the mirror at her. 'You still are,' he murmured, bending down so that his chin rested in her hair. She felt his hands sliding down over her breasts, and the difference in the sensation compared with when Chris had touched her was vast. This was a caress, an expression of feeling, and she pressed herself against him.

'Let me love you again,' he begged, unfastening the tie of the blouse.

'I don't think . . .'

'I don't want you to think,' he said sharply, and then he was lifting her up and carrying her towards the bed. He unfastened her blouse but left it on so that her breasts thrust out through the opening. Looking into his eyes she knew without doubt that she'd been right. He did love her, and he desperately wanted her to love him in return.

Slowly and sensuously he unfastened her Indian cotton skirt and eased it over her hips. She was naked beneath it and he pressed his mouth to her pubic mound while his hands moved upwards along the sides of her body.

Harriet's breathing quickened and she knew that she was going to respond, to accept his lovemaking with gratitude because this was what she wanted. However it had started out, she knew that by the time it ended she had emerged the winner.

Lewis stripped off his own clothes and then sat at the top of the bed, his back supported by the headrest. His erection stood up proudly and without taking his eyes from Harriet, he let himself slide down the bed until he was flat on his back with his knees raised.

Once he was still, Harriet climbed on top of him. She positioned her knees on either side of him and lowered herself on to his erection, allowing him to enter her very slowly, a fraction of an inch at a time. Whenever he tried to move she would raise herself so that he slid out of her again.

Lewis quickly realised what he had to do and forced himself to lie still until at last he was fully inside her. 'Lean back against my legs,' he whispered. Harriet did, and when Lewis shifted slightly this meant that he was penetrating her as deeply as possible.

'I'm going to bring myself to a climax,' she murmured, staring directly into his eyes. 'You mustn't come before me.'

'And what will happen if I do?' he asked with a smile.

'I shall leave, like I said before,' she replied.

The smile faded from his face. 'Harriet, don't joke about it.'

'I'm not joking. You've played enough sexual games with me. I thought you might like to experience one for yourself. I'm sure your legendary self-control will come to your assistance.'

Lewis wasn't so certain. His testicles were already drawn up tightly against his body and there was a dangerous tingling sensation in his glans which meant that his orgasm was very near.

'You have to watch me,' insisted Harriet when he closed his eyes.

Lewis obeyed, and watched as she parted her outer sex-lips, revealing herself fully to him. His mouth went dry when her fingers carefully spread the inner lips apart and then she was running one finger along the shiny delicate pink flesh of her inner channel.

Harriet forgot the man beneath her, forgot how hard he was struggling for control, all she could think about was the rising tide of sexual heat.

Suddenly she held out her hand to Lewis. 'Lick my finger,' she said breathlessly. He flicked out his tongue and tasted the delicious tang of her arousal. With a smile she returned the saliva-moistened fingertip between her thighs and let it move in slow circles around her clitoris.

Lewis felt that he would explode at the sight. Her eyelids were heavy, her cheeks flushed, her whole body taut and ready for the climax she was instigating. The tingling in his glans increased and his hips twitched slightly.

'Not yet,' whispered Harriet, remembering the times he'd made her wait for satisfaction.

Lewis groaned. He was certain he couldn't control himself much longer, but now Harriet was moving her free hand behind her and as one hand continued to tease her clitoris and surrounding flesh the other lightly tickled his swollen testicles.

'Harriet, no!' he begged.

She smiled to herself at the expression of anguish on his face, and then her clitoris began to throb and suddenly her own climax took over and her body tightened so that she knew release was only seconds away.

Lewis knew it too and prayed she'd hurry because he'd never been balanced on the edge of gratification for so long before. To his relief her body abruptly bent forward as the first muscular contractions took hold of her and then she was twisting and turning on his erection as she cried out with pleasure and release.

Now Lewis too could come and he thrust forcefully upwards, knowing that he was filling every inch of her and as her orgasm began to wane he moved her roughly up and down on him. Her sensitive nerve endings were reactivated and as his hot seed exploded into her she climaxed again, shuddering and moaning until at last they were both still.

Lewis helped her off him and drew her down to lie on top of him. 'Does that mean you won't leave me?' he asked at last.

'Not yet,' she said with a smile.

'We'll go back to the States. Rowena and I will get

divorced, the marriage was really over long ago. There's so much I want to show you.'

'I've enjoyed your film,' she said softly. 'If it's a success, will you repeat the experiment?'

'Using other characters, you mean?

'Some of them could be new, but sequels are popular. Maybe the fictional Harriet and her lover could figure in the next one too.'

Lewis nodded in appreciation. 'I think that sounds a very good idea. You'll have to give me time to think about it though. Besides, the first film might not be a success.'

Harriet ran her hands over his chest, tweaking his sensitive nipples. 'I'm sure it will be. How could it fail with so many twists in the plot?'

'A good question,' agreed Lewis, wrapping his arms around her. He loved her, yes, but already his thoughts were on the film, the script and now the incredibly exciting possibility of using Harriet in another piece of *cinéma verité*.

'What will happen to Rowena and Chris?' asked Harriet as she drifted off to sleep.

'I don't think we have to worry about them,' replied Lewis. 'When I passed Chris's door it sounded as though they were both very active. I imagine they'll stay here in England and live their life behind closed doors, the way they've always wanted to.'

The one thing Harriet knew for sure was that she must never let Lewis become complacent about her. He was a man who liked a challenge, and although she sensed that her need for him was just as great as his was for her she didn't intend to let him know that.

'I hope I like America,' she said, trying to suppress a yawn. 'I should do. As long as I don't get bored.'

'I won't let you get bored,' promised Lewis, snuggling up behind her so that they fitted together like two spoons. 'I have some very exciting things in mind for us both.'

Harriet smiled to herself. She hoped he had because she knew that in some ways Chris had been right. There was still a lot that her body wanted to learn, and if Lewis wouldn't teach her then hopefully he'd make sure they got involved with people who would.

Epilogue

'*I CAN'T BELIEVE* it!' exclaimed Mark, watching Lewis adjust his bow tie in front of the mirror.

Lewis frowned. 'What can't you believe? The fact that I'm getting married again?'

Mark laughed. 'That's the one thing that does make sense. If Harriet had ever given me so much as a second glance I'd have snapped her up, I can tell you.'

'Lucky for me she didn't then!' exclaimed Lewis wryly.

'I meant the film's success,' Mark continued. 'You're the first director ever to make an art film and turn it into a massive mainstream box office hit.'

'If you'd known what was going to happen perhaps you wouldn't have made such a fuss about the ending when you were writing it,' said Lewis. 'I nearly had to type the last scene myself if I remember correctly.'

'It just wasn't what I'd expected,' protested Mark. 'But you were right, as usual.'

'We'd better go down,' said Lewis. 'I can hardly be late for Harriet because I'm talking business on our wedding day!'

They went down the massive staircase of his Beverly Hills mansion and out on to the lawn where over two hundred guests were assembled.

'Have you thought any more about a sequel?' asked Mark.

'Today you're meant to be my best man, not my scriptwriter.'

'But have you?'

Lewis glanced at his watch. 'Harriet's late. How many hours does it take to put on a wedding dress?'

'A bride's always late. Have you?' persisted Mark.

'Of course I have.'

'And?'

Lewis glanced anxiously towards the house. 'Where is she?'

Mark put a hand on his arm. 'She isn't going to run away, you know! Relax. Tell me about the sequel.'

Running his hands through his dark hair Lewis gave in. It was better than fretting in case Harriet had changed her mind. It had been difficult enough to persuade her to marry him. Now that the wheels were all in motion it would be disastrous if she changed her mind.

'At the start of the film, Helena – our heroine from *Dark Secret* – is getting married,' he said slowly. Mark stared at him, his eyes suddenly alert. 'Her husband's still a workaholic, and they go away on their honeymoon with a business colleague and his wife of ten years. The colleague, who's also a friend, lusts after Helena and has done ever since he first set eyes on her.'

'Does the husband know this?' asked Mark.

Lewis smiled. 'Of course. But he knows, you see, that his new wife needs excitement and new experiences if she's to be really happy so he encourages her to get to know his friend very well indeed.'

'What's the friend like?' asked Mark.

'On the surface an extremely courteous and charming Englishman. Underneath it's a rather different story.'

'And what happens?' asked Mark.

Lewis shrugged. 'Who knows? I'll probably mail you the first few scenes while we're away.'

'You're not working on your honeymoon!'

'Here she is!' exclaimed Lewis. 'Doesn't she look incredible?'

Mark looked towards the house and saw Harriet gliding across the lawn towards them. She was wearing an elegant straight white dress in taffeta with a lace bodice and peplum, enhanced by a taffeta sash. In her hands she held a spray of salmon and white rosebuds and matching flowers were entwined in her gossamer-fine headdress.

'She looks fantastic!' agreed Mark.

Throughout the ceremony Lewis never took his eyes off her. Later as they mingled with the guests, most of whom were strangers to Harriet, he kept her hand imprisoned tightly in his as though he was terrified she'd disappear if he released her.

Harriet was relieved when they finally found themselves alone for a brief moment. Lewis had drawn her into his study, ostensibly so that she could freshen up her makeup, but the moment they were alone he began kissing her passionately, pressing his body urgently against hers and murmuring incoherently in her ear.

She was overwhelmed by love for him and let her head fall back so that he could kiss and nibble at the soft white skin of her throat.

'Say you love me!' he said fiercely.

'You know I do,' responded Harriet, her knees trembling at the thought of the passion they'd be sharing on their honeymoon.

'Say it!' he repeated. 'You never actually say the words.'

'I love you, Lewis,' she whispered.

He gave a sigh of satisfaction. 'I know I've neglected you over the past few weeks, but I've been so busy. Once we get away it will be different.'

'I understand,' she assured him.

Lewis straightened her headdress and teased a strand of hair down over her forehead. 'There, that looks better, much sexier!' Laughing she took his hand again and they went out into the hallway.

A man was standing there, examining one of Lewis's paintings. When he heard the study door open he turned and smiled at the couple.

'Edmund!' exclaimed Lewis, holding out a hand. 'Now nice to see you. Harriet, I don't believe you've met Edmund, have you? He's one of my closest friends, and more importantly a fervent supporter of my work. He's putting the money up for the next film.'

'The sequel to *Dark Secret?*' she asked.

'Yes.'

'Hardly a high-risk project then,' laughed Harriet.

The man smiled at her. 'No, but I did back *Dark Secret* as well, and that certainly was a risk so I think I'm entitled to a less worrying investment this time round!'

His voice surprised Harriet. She'd grown used to Americans now, but he was clearly an Englishman with the beautifully modulated tones of an expensively educated one.

'You're English too!' she laughed.

He nodded. 'We'll have to form an alliance, Harriet.'

Something in the way he spoke caught her attention, and Harriet looked at him more carefully. He was tall, although not as tall as Lewis, and very slim with brown curly hair, dark eyes and an extremely sensuous mouth.

'I'd like that,' she said slowly.

At that moment a very tall blonde woman came in from the garden and slipped her arm through Edmund's. 'There you are, sweetie! I've been looking all over for you.'

'Harriet, this is my wife Noella. Noella, I'm sure you recognise Lewis's lovely bride.'

'Sure I do. Welcome to Beverly Hills, honey.'

'Do you miss England?' asked Edmund, his eyes warm.

'Yes, desperately,' confessed Harriet. 'That's why Lewis is taking me back there for our honeymoon.'

'Is that right? Whereabouts are you staying?' asked Noella.

'Cornwall,' said Lewis. 'I've always wanted to see it, and Harriet spent a lot of time there as a child.'

'What a coincidence,' cried Noella, glancing at her husband. 'We're off to Cornwall next week too.'

'It's hardly a coincidence,' said her husband quietly. 'Lewis and I have a lot to discuss over the next few weeks. It seemed sensible for us to be close so I decided to combine our long-awaited trip with his honeymoon.'

Harriet stared at Edmund and then back at her husband. 'You mean you're going to work on our honeymoon?'

He squeezed her hand. 'I wouldn't really call it work, sweetheart. Edmund and I need to finalise a few details concerning the sequel. I know how interested you are in that, so I didn't think you'd mind.'

A thrill of excitement ran through Harriet. Now she understood what Lewis had meant when he'd told her that their honeymoon would be something she'd never forget. She looked at Edmund again. He was definitely attractive, and she sensed that beneath the urbane surface there was much more to him than met the eye.

'You don't mind, do you, Harriet?' he asked with a half-smile.

Harriet shook her head and looked up at her new husband. 'I can hardly wait,' she assured him. Lewis bent his head and kissed her full on the lips.

Edmund stood watching silently for a moment and then turned and left with Noella. He was content. His turn would come.